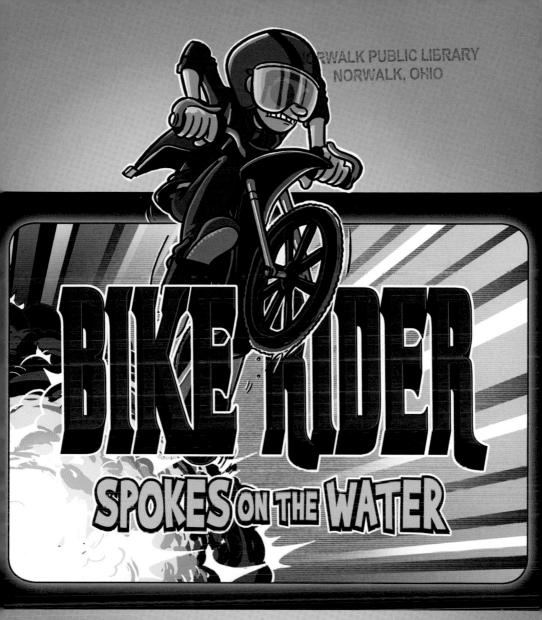

BIKE RIDER

SPOKES ON THE WATER

created by **Donnie Lemke** & **Douglas Holgate**

STONE ARCH BOOKS
a capstone imprint

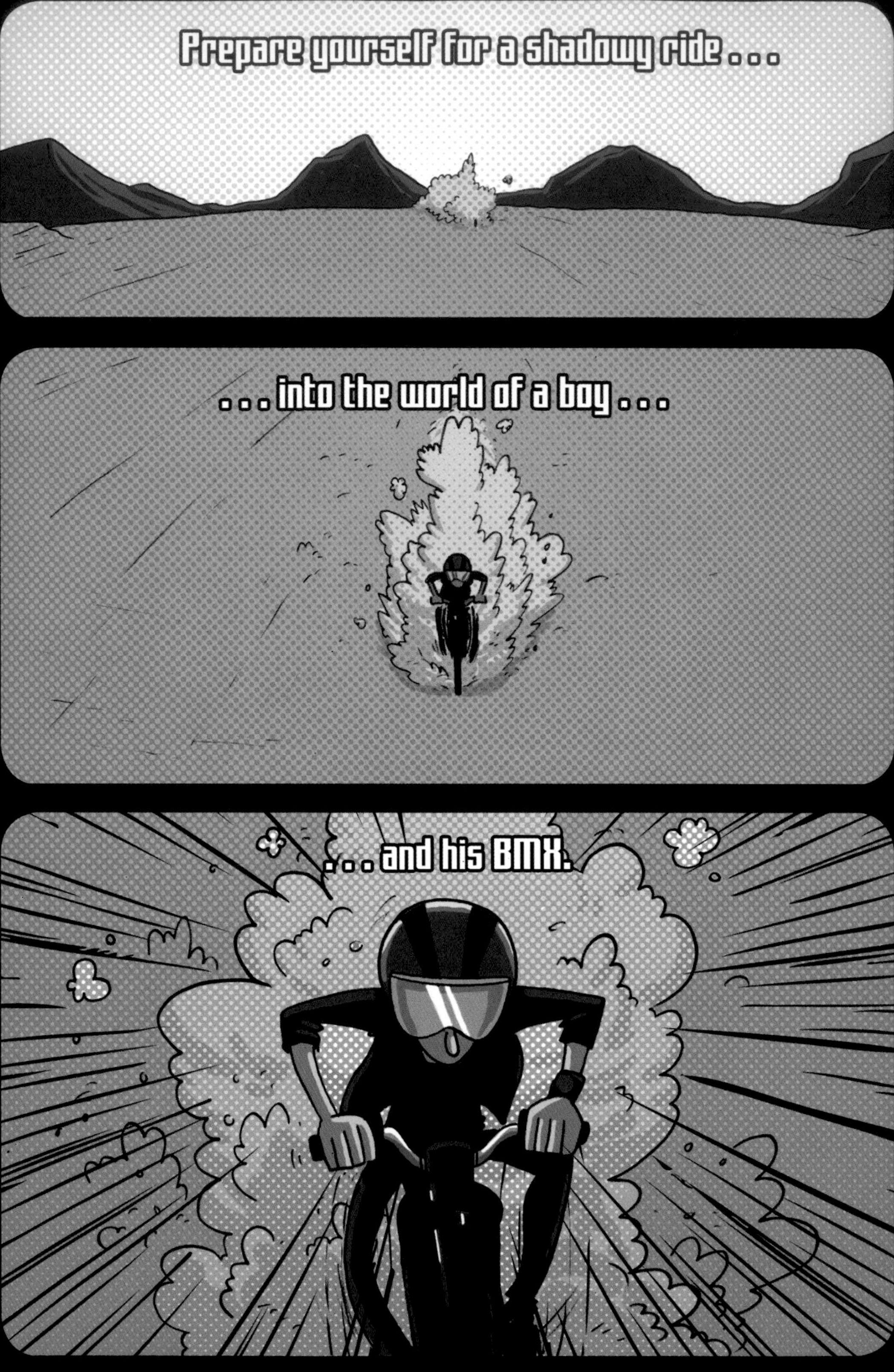
Prepare yourself for a shadowy ride . . .
. . . into the world of a boy . . .
. . . and his BMX.

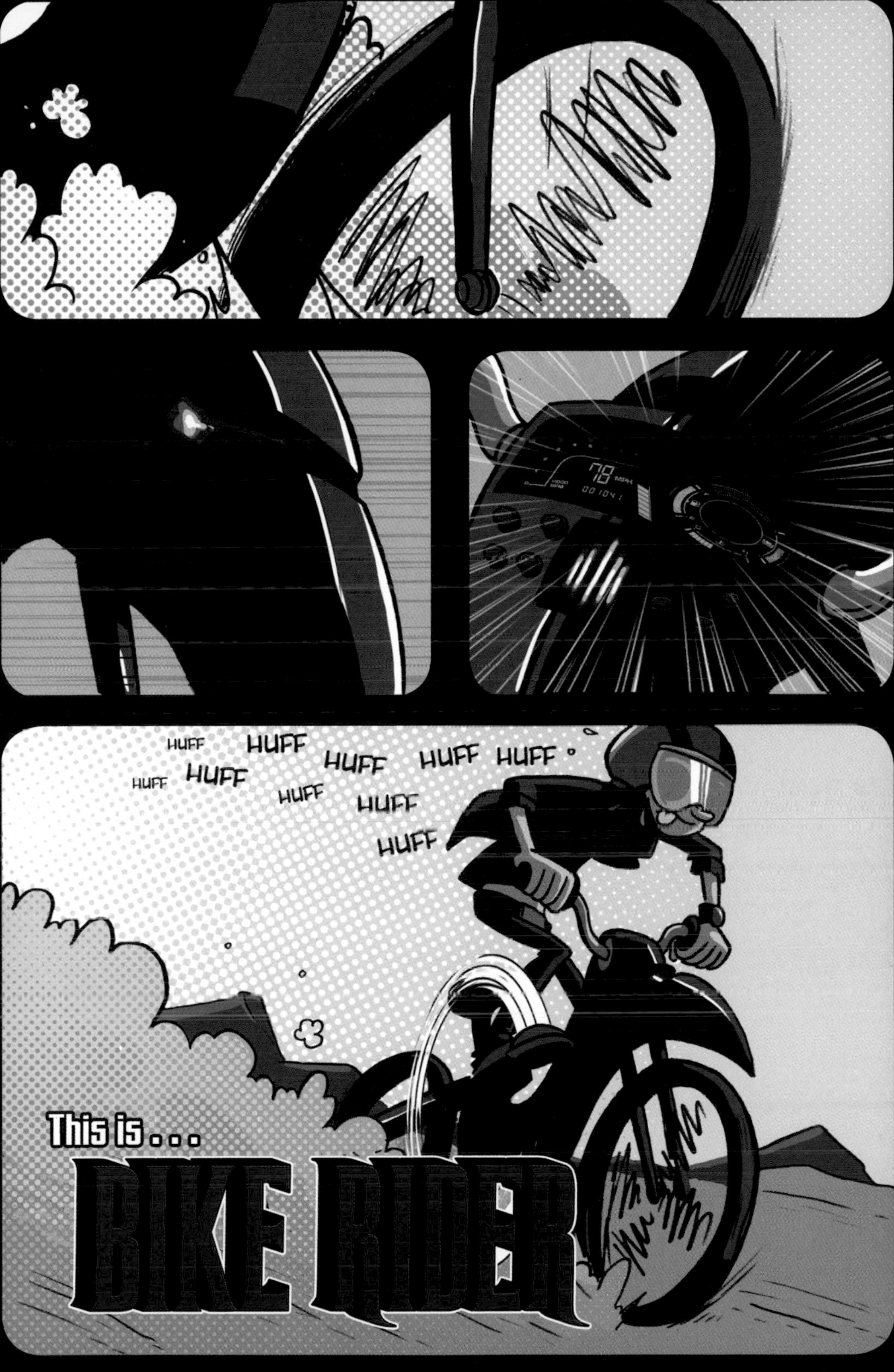
78 MPH
001041
HUFF HUFF HUFF HUFF HUFF HUFF HUFF HUFF HUFF HUFF
This is . . .
BIKE RIDER

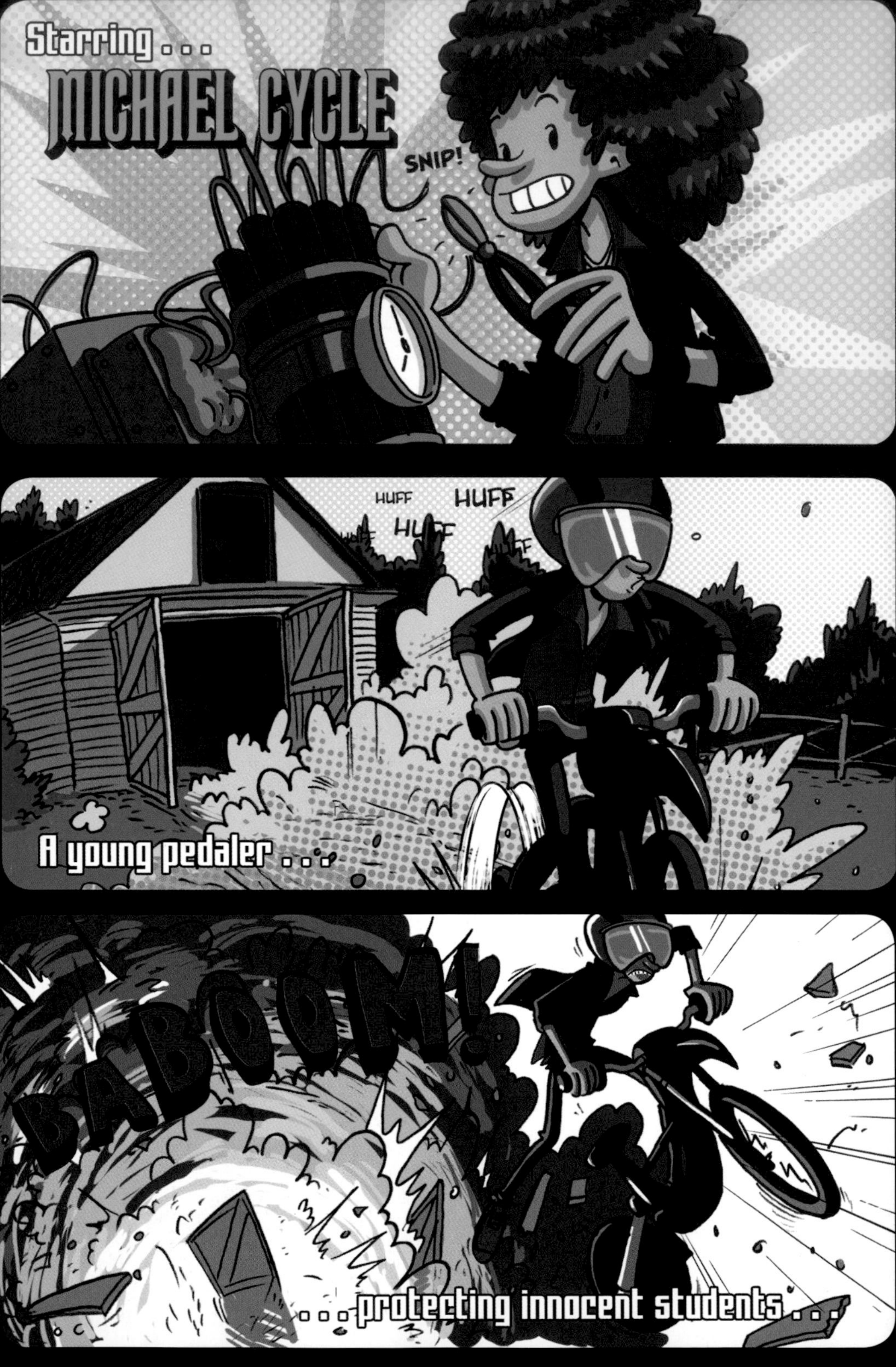
Starring . . .
MICHAEL CYCLE
SNIP!
HUFF
HUFF
HUFF
A young pedaler . . .
BABOOM!
. . . protecting innocent students . . .

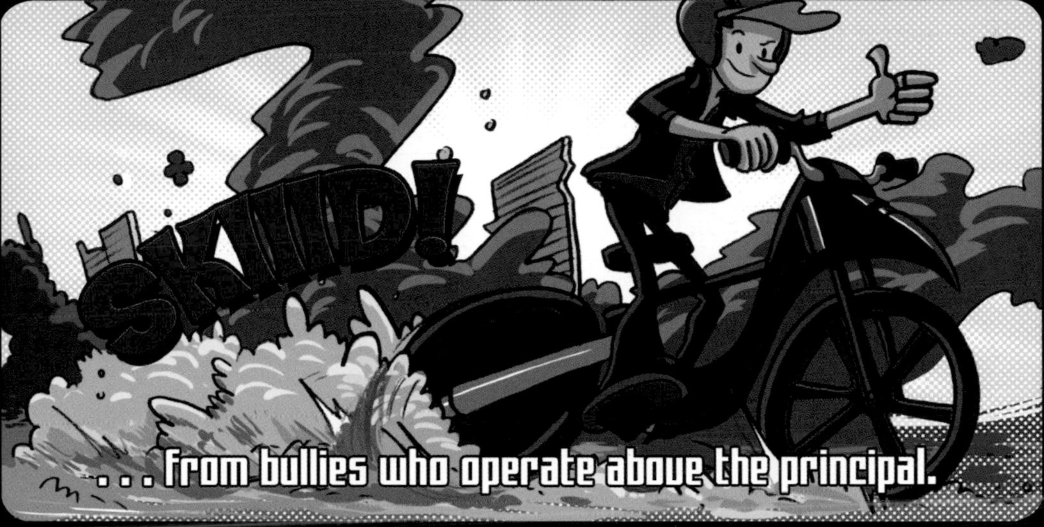
SKIIID!
. . . from bullies who operate above the principal.

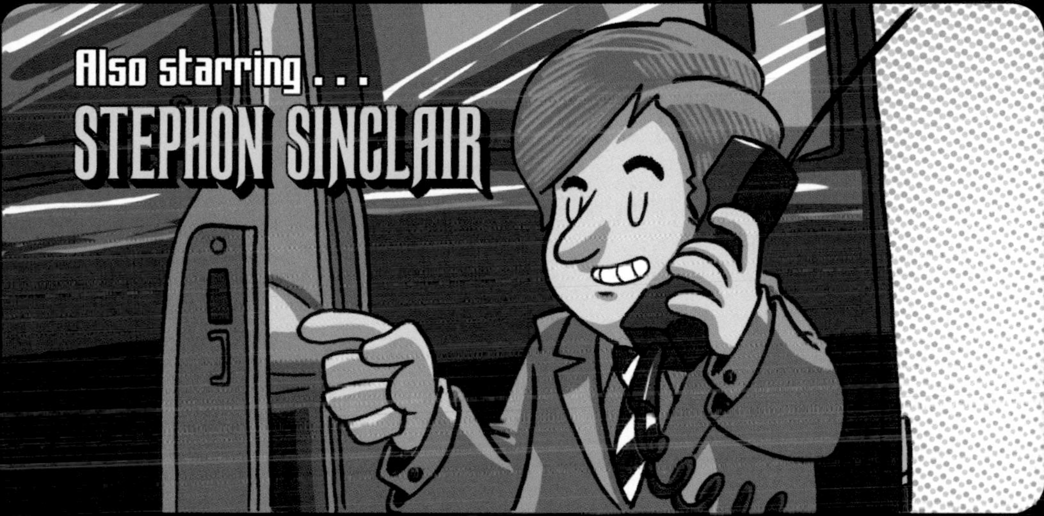
Also starring . . .
STEPHON SINCLAIR

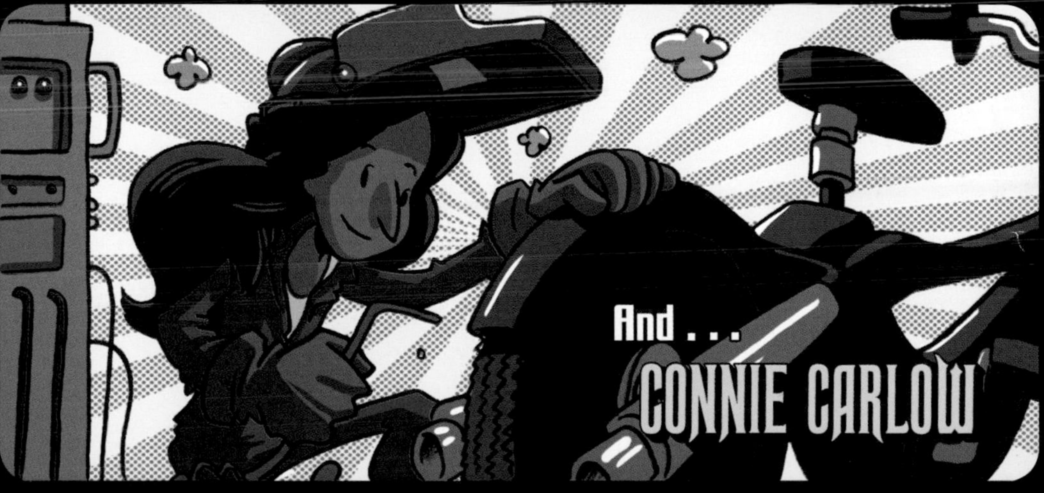
And . . .
CONNIE CARLOW

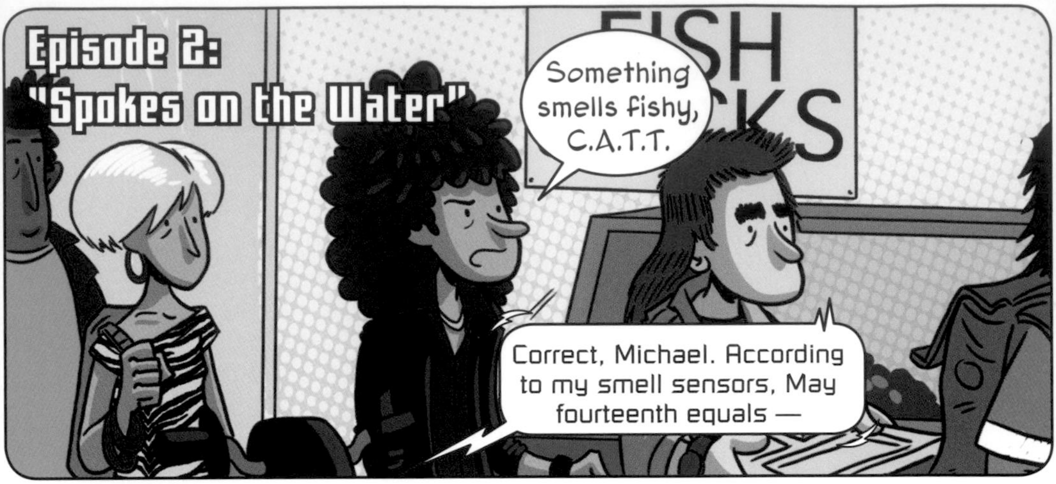
Episode 2:
"Spokes on the Water"
FISH STICKS
Something smells fishy, C.A.T.T.
Correct, Michael. According to my smell sensors, May fourteenth equals —

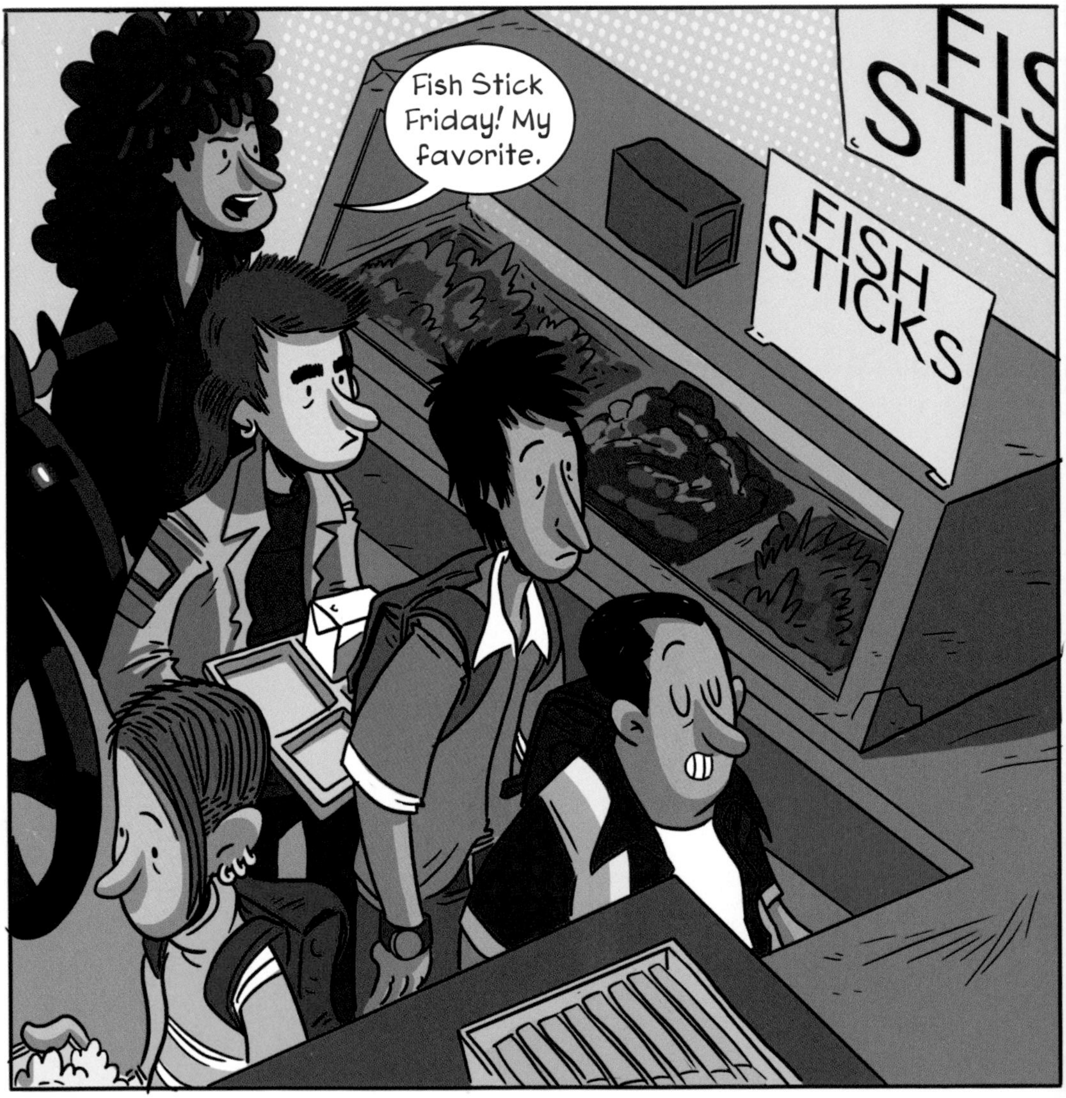
Fish Stick Friday! My favorite.
FISH STICKS
FISH STICKS

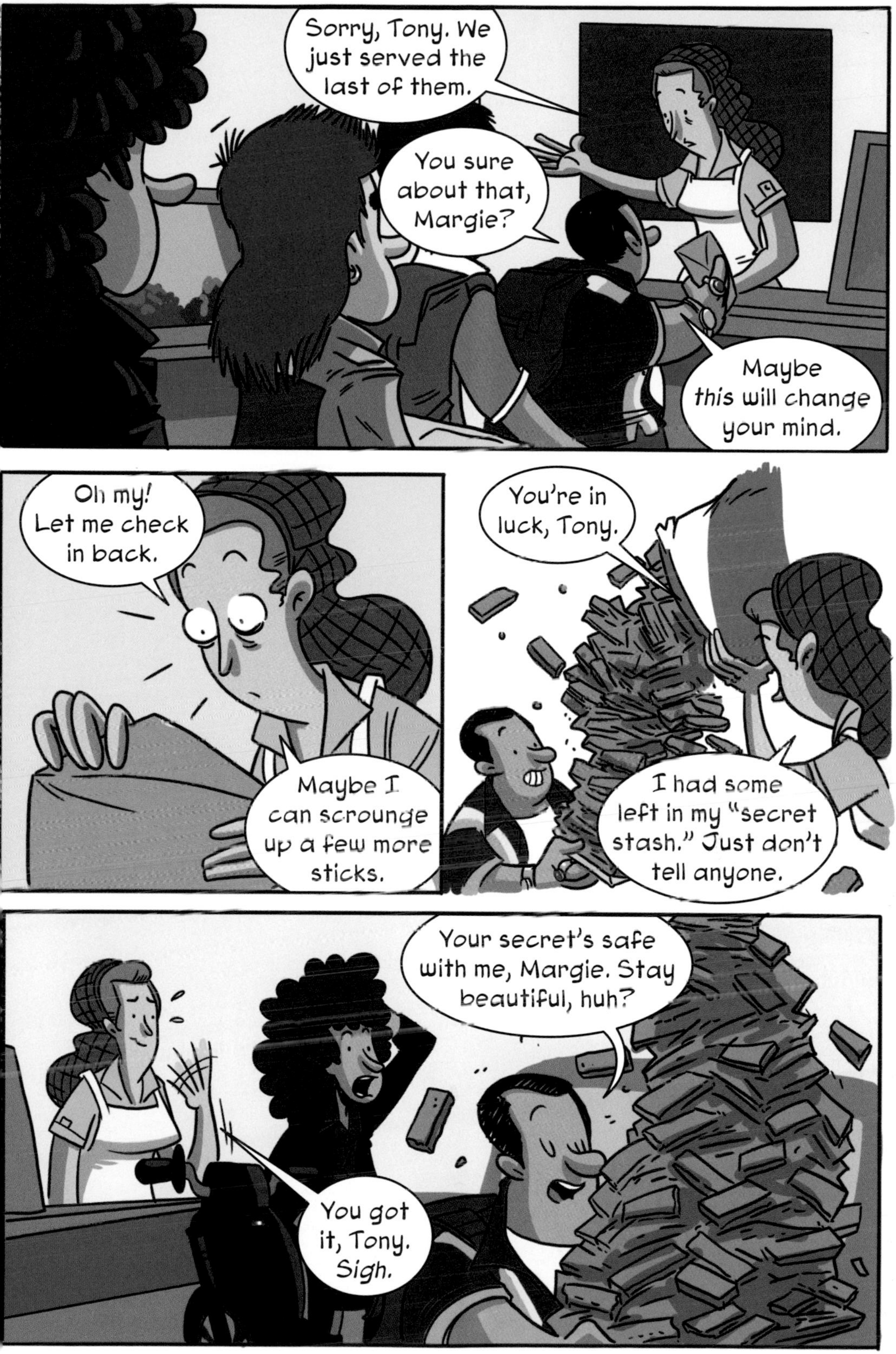
Sorry, Tony. We just served the last of them.
You sure about that, Margie?
Maybe *this* will change your mind.
Oh my! Let me check in back.
Maybe I can scrounge up a few more sticks.
You're in luck, Tony.
I had some left in my "secret stash." Just don't tell anyone.
Your secret's safe with me, Margie. Stay beautiful, huh?
You got it, Tony. Sigh.

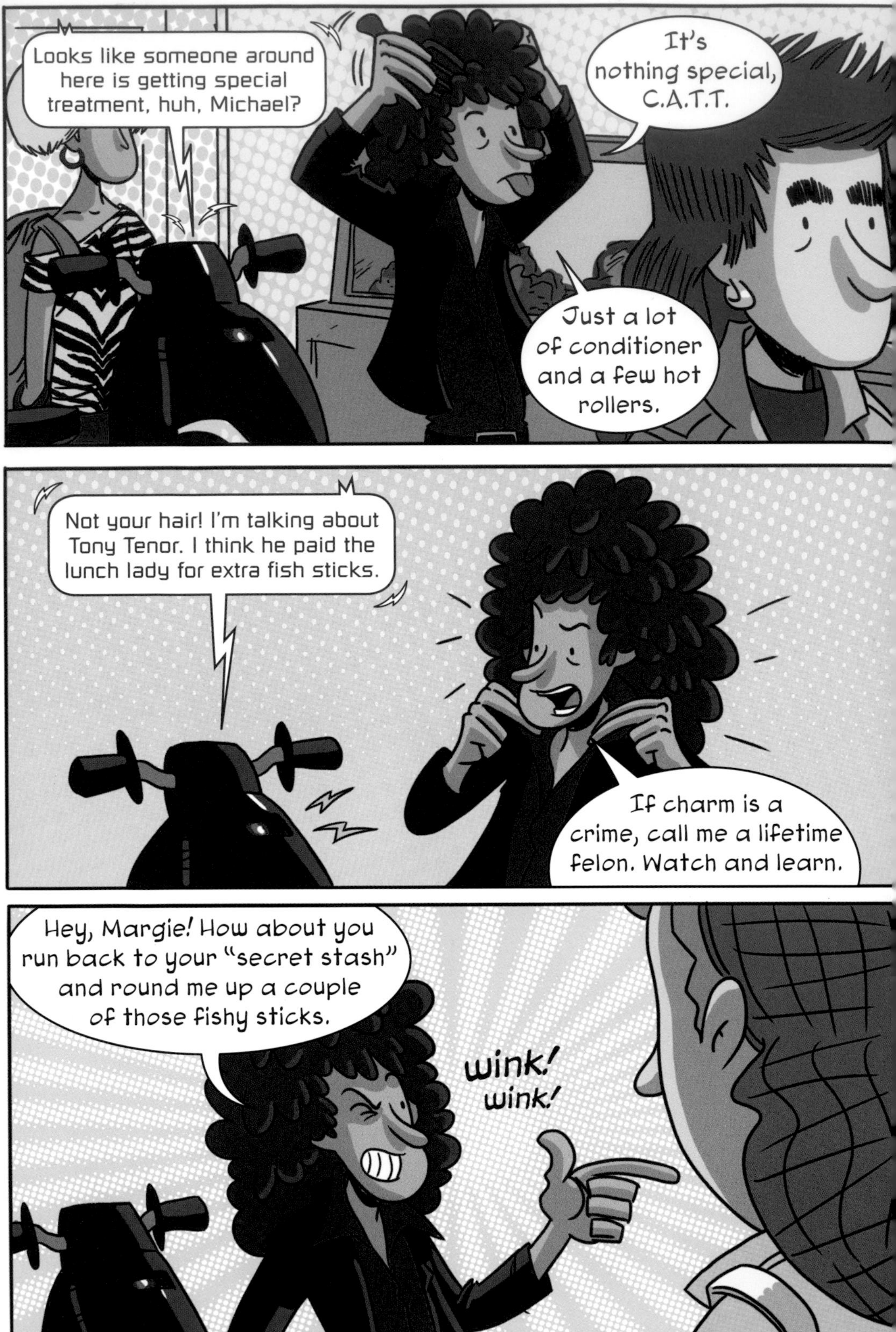
Looks like someone around here is getting special treatment, huh, Michael?
It's nothing special, C.A.T.T.
Just a lot of conditioner and a few hot rollers.
Not your hair! I'm talking about Tony Tenor. I think he paid the lunch lady for extra fish sticks.
If charm is a crime, call me a lifetime felon. Watch and learn.
Hey, Margie! How about you run back to your "secret stash" and round me up a couple of those fishy sticks.
wink!
wink!

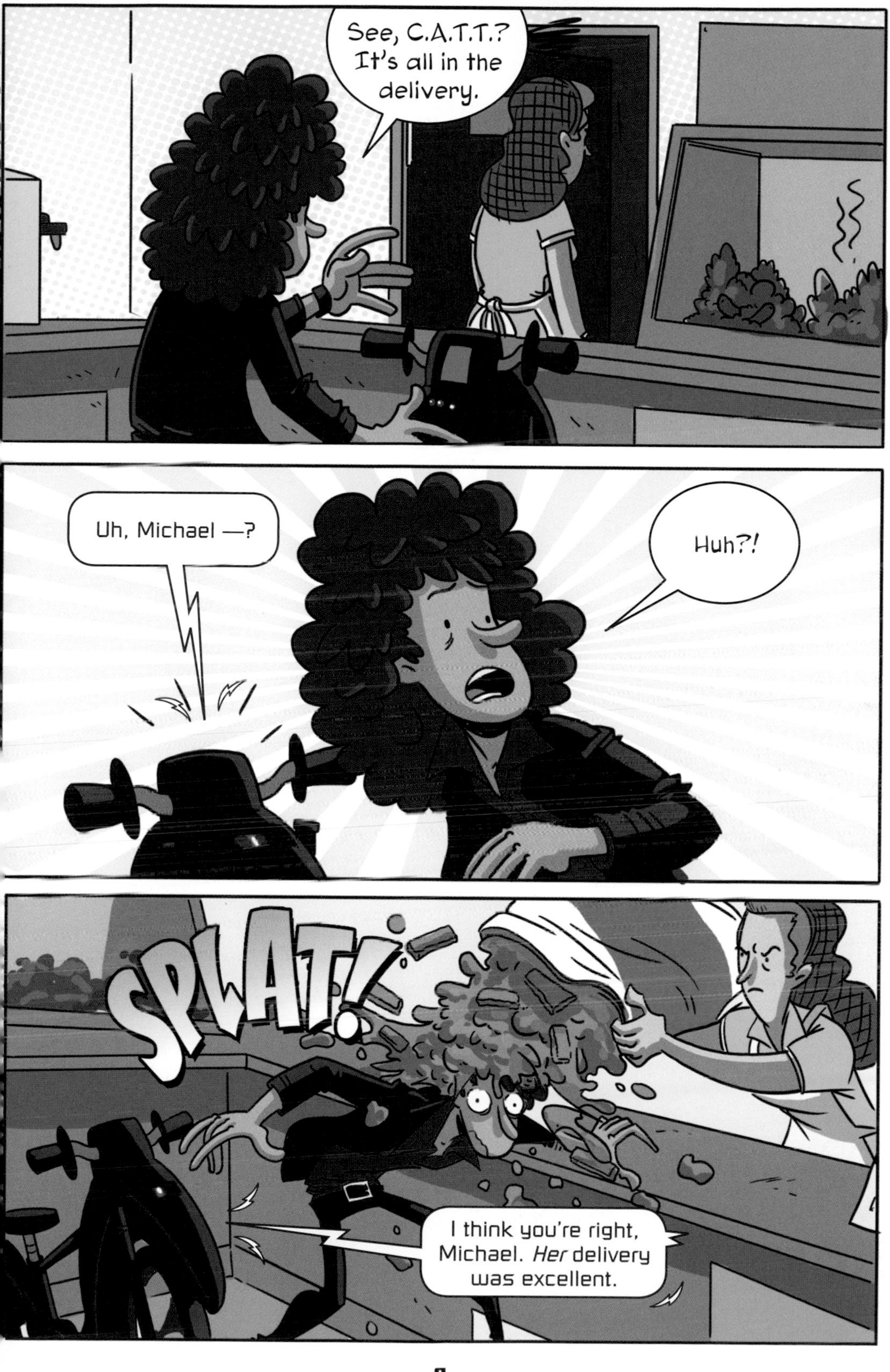

See, C.A.T.T.? It's all in the delivery.
Uh, Michael —?
Huh?!
SPLAT!
I think you're right, Michael. *Her* delivery was excellent.

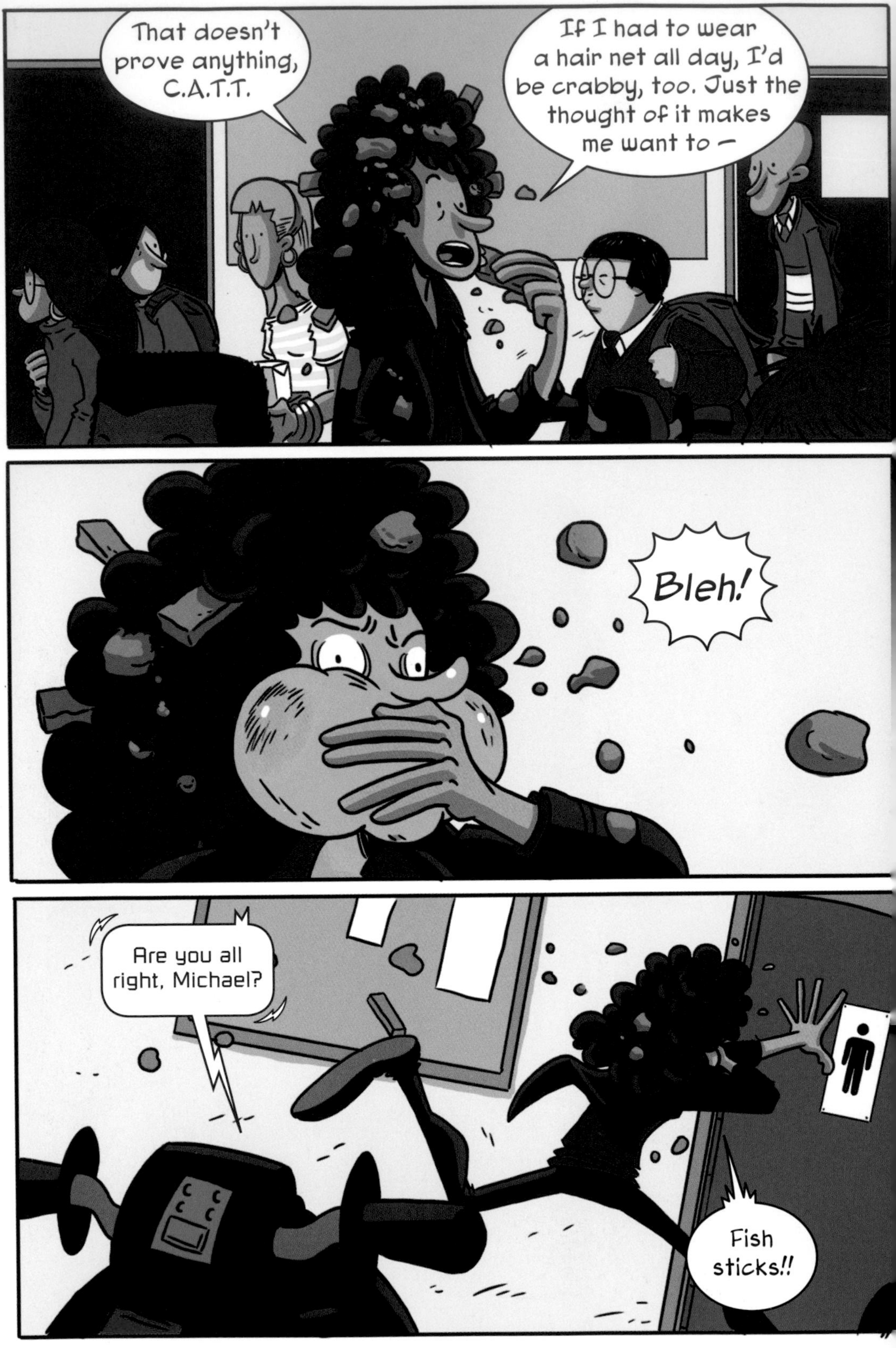
That doesn't prove anything, C.A.T.T.
If I had to wear a hair net all day, I'd be crabby, too. Just the thought of it makes me want to —
Bleh!
Are you all right, Michael?
Fish sticks!!

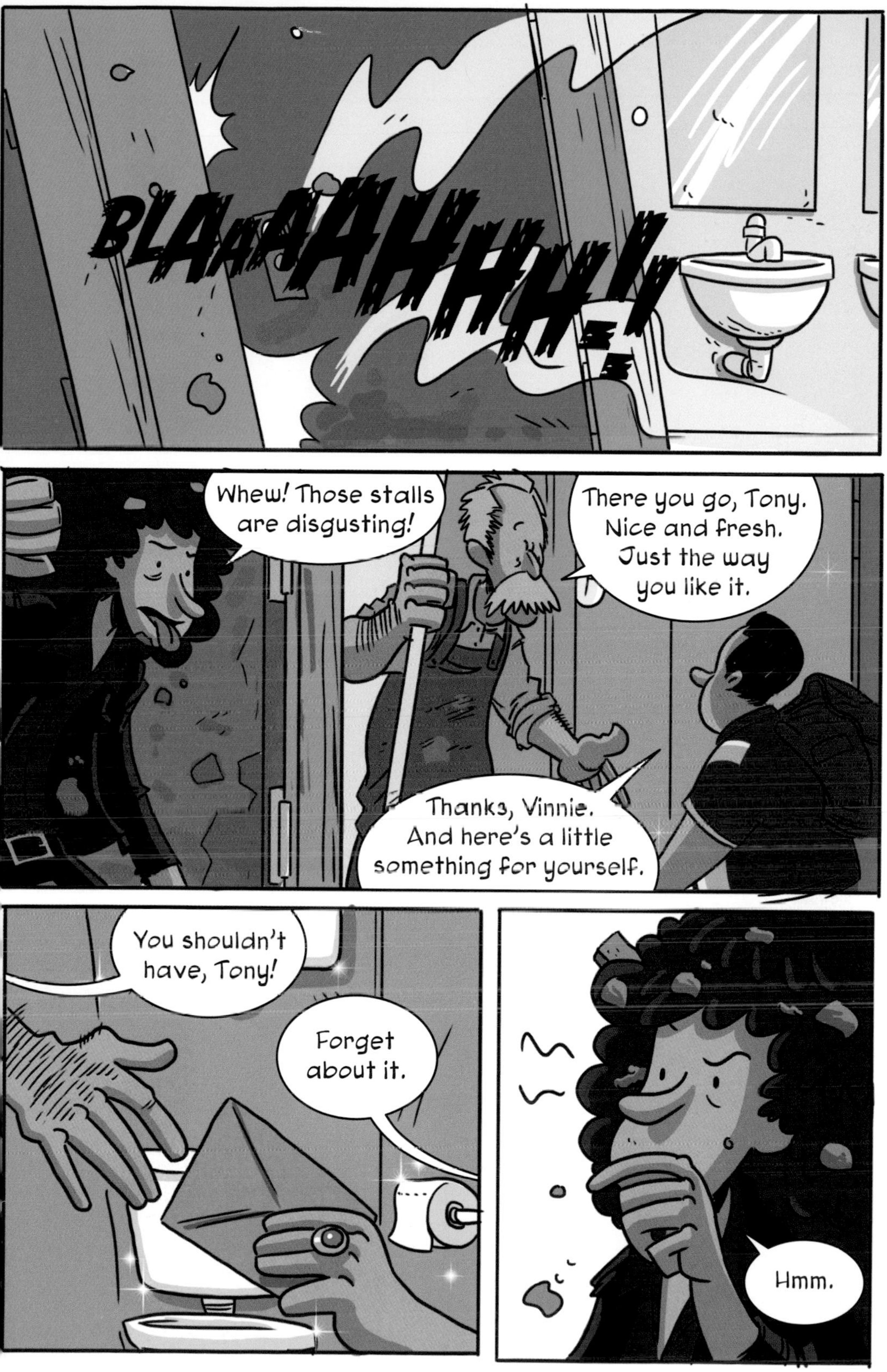
BLAAAAHHHH!!
Whew! Those stalls are disgusting!
There you go, Tony. Nice and fresh. Just the way you like it.
Thanks, Vinnie. And here's a little something for yourself.
You shouldn't have, Tony!
Forget about it.
Hmm.

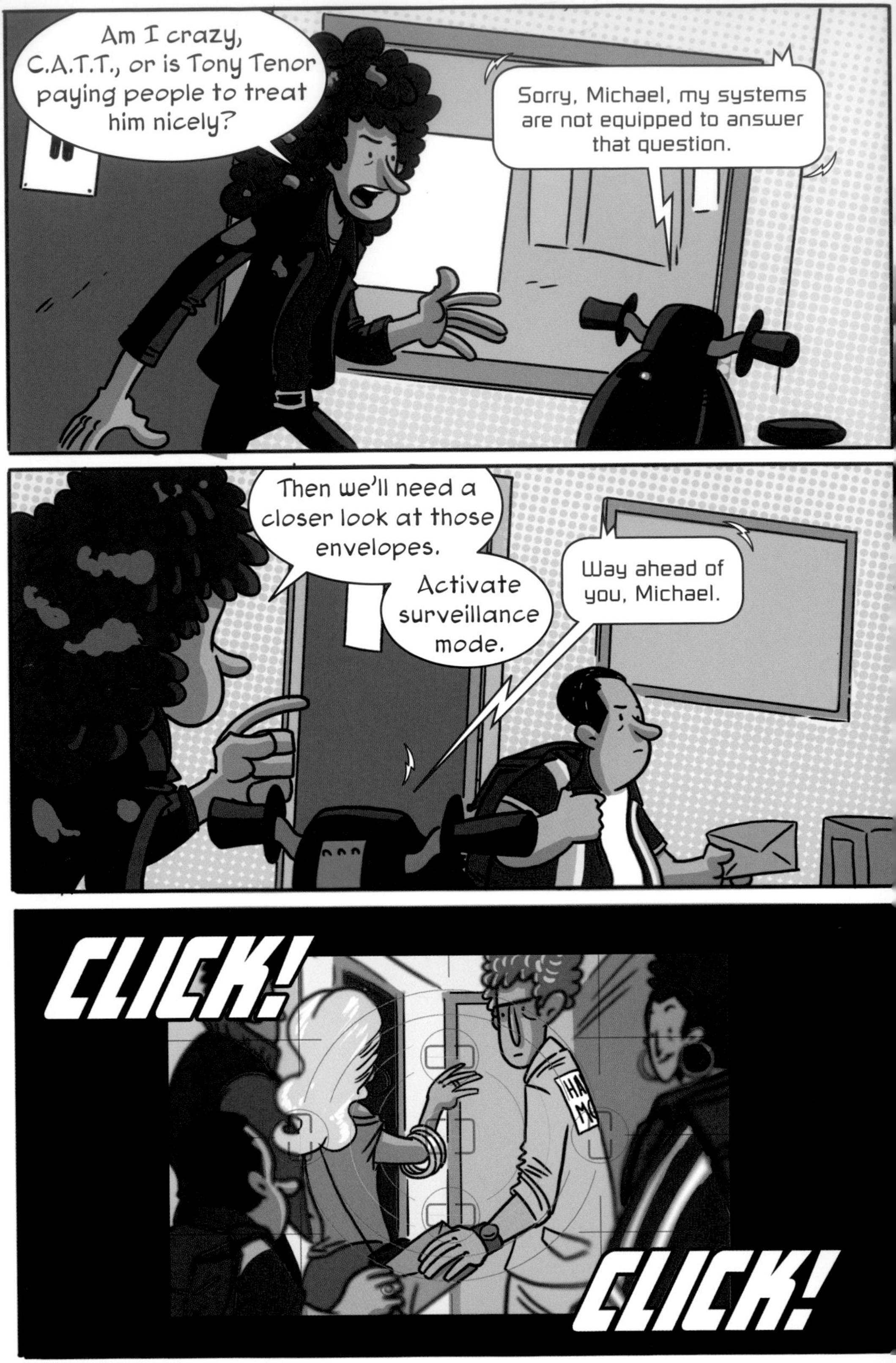
Am I crazy, C.A.T.T., or is Tony Tenor paying people to treat him nicely?
Sorry, Michael, my systems are not equipped to answer that question.
Then we'll need a closer look at those envelopes.
Activate surveillance mode.
Way ahead of you, Michael.
CLICK!
CLICK!

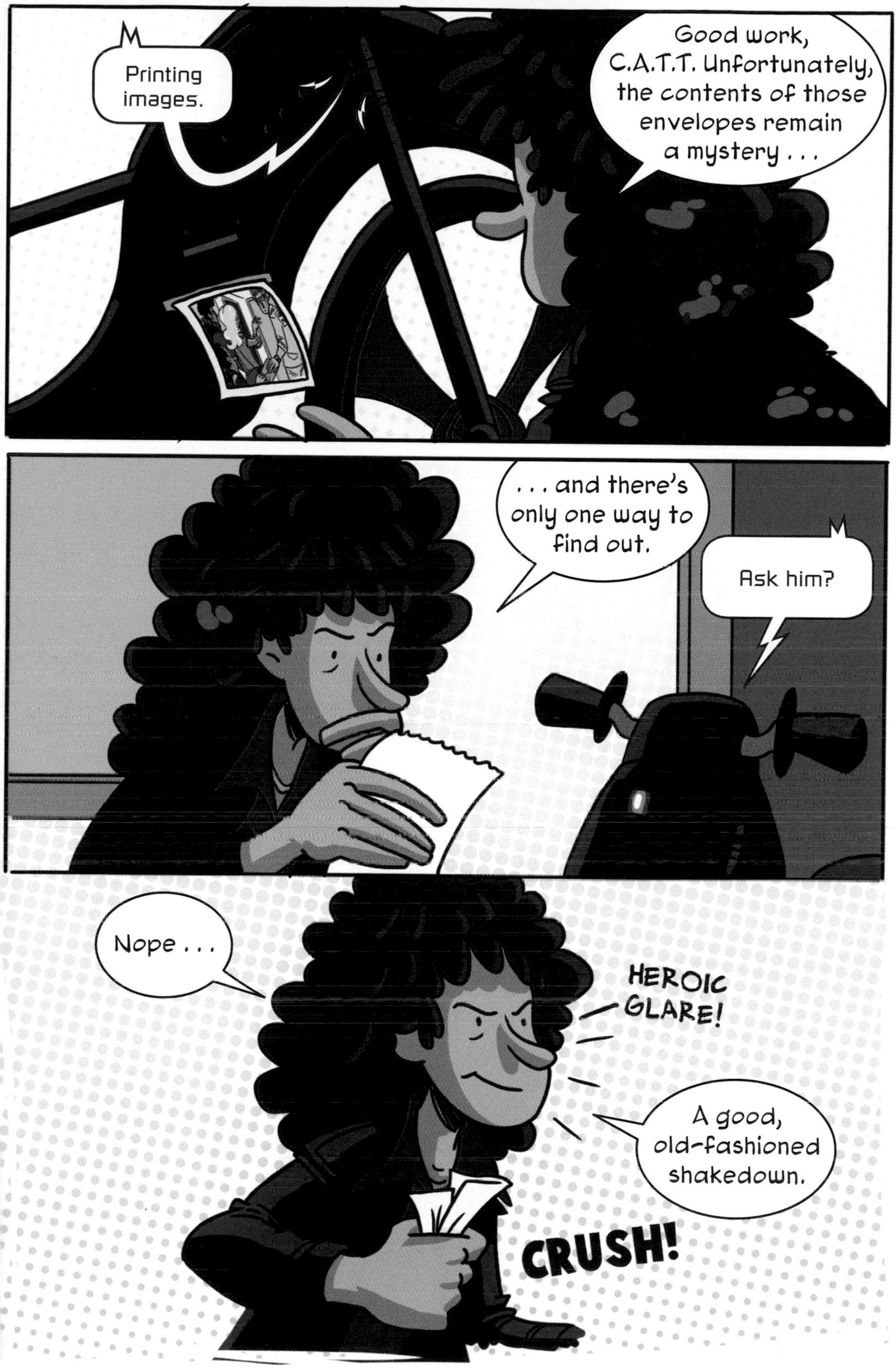
Printing images.
Good work, C.A.T.T. Unfortunately, the contents of those envelopes remain a mystery . . .
. . . and there's only one way to find out.
Ask him?
Nope . . .
HEROIC GLARE!
A good, old-fashioned shakedown.
CRUSH!

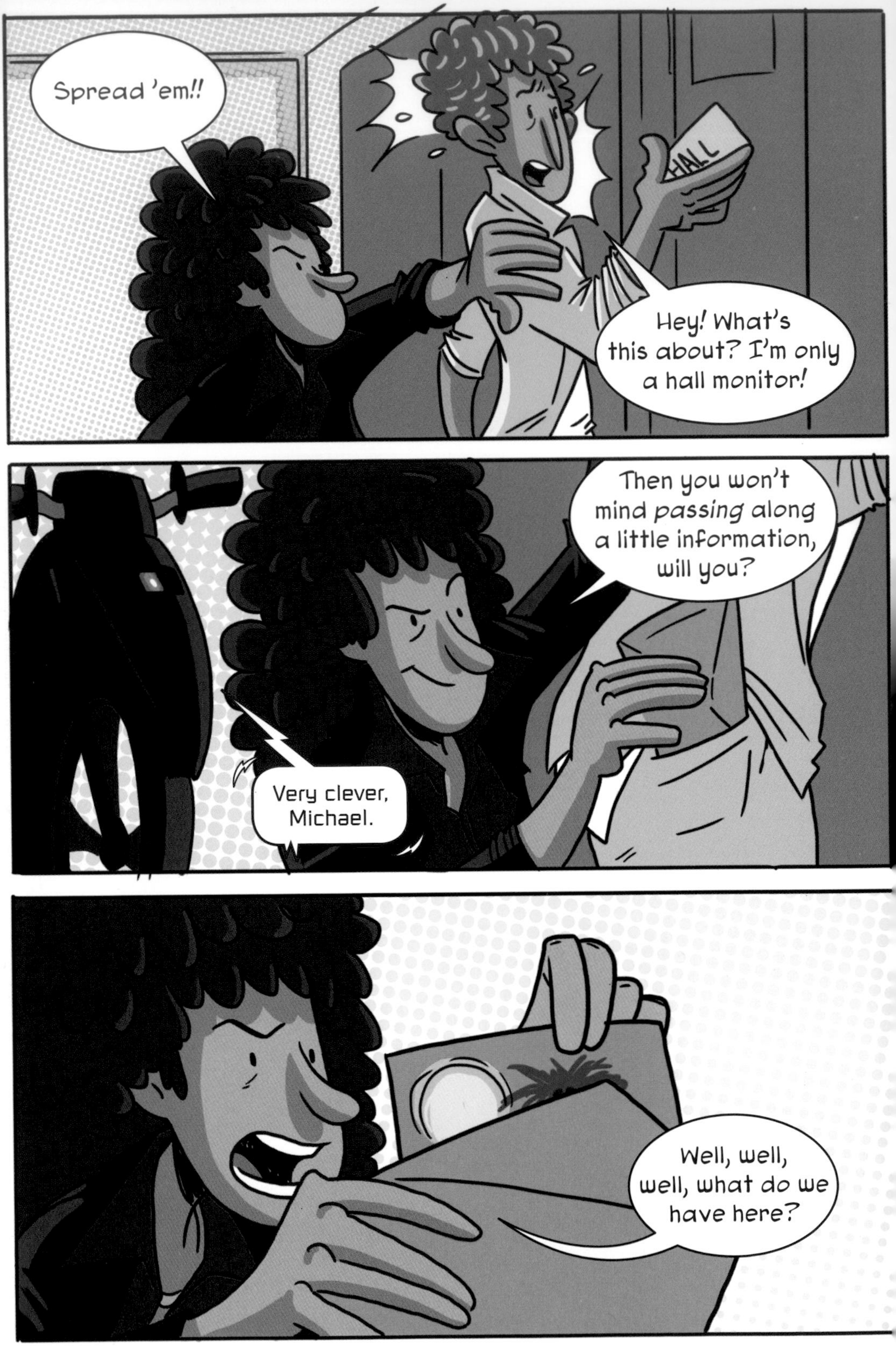
Spread 'em!!
Hey! What's this about? I'm only a hall monitor!
HALL
Then you won't mind *passing* along a little information, will you?
Very clever, Michael.
Well, well, well, what do we have here?

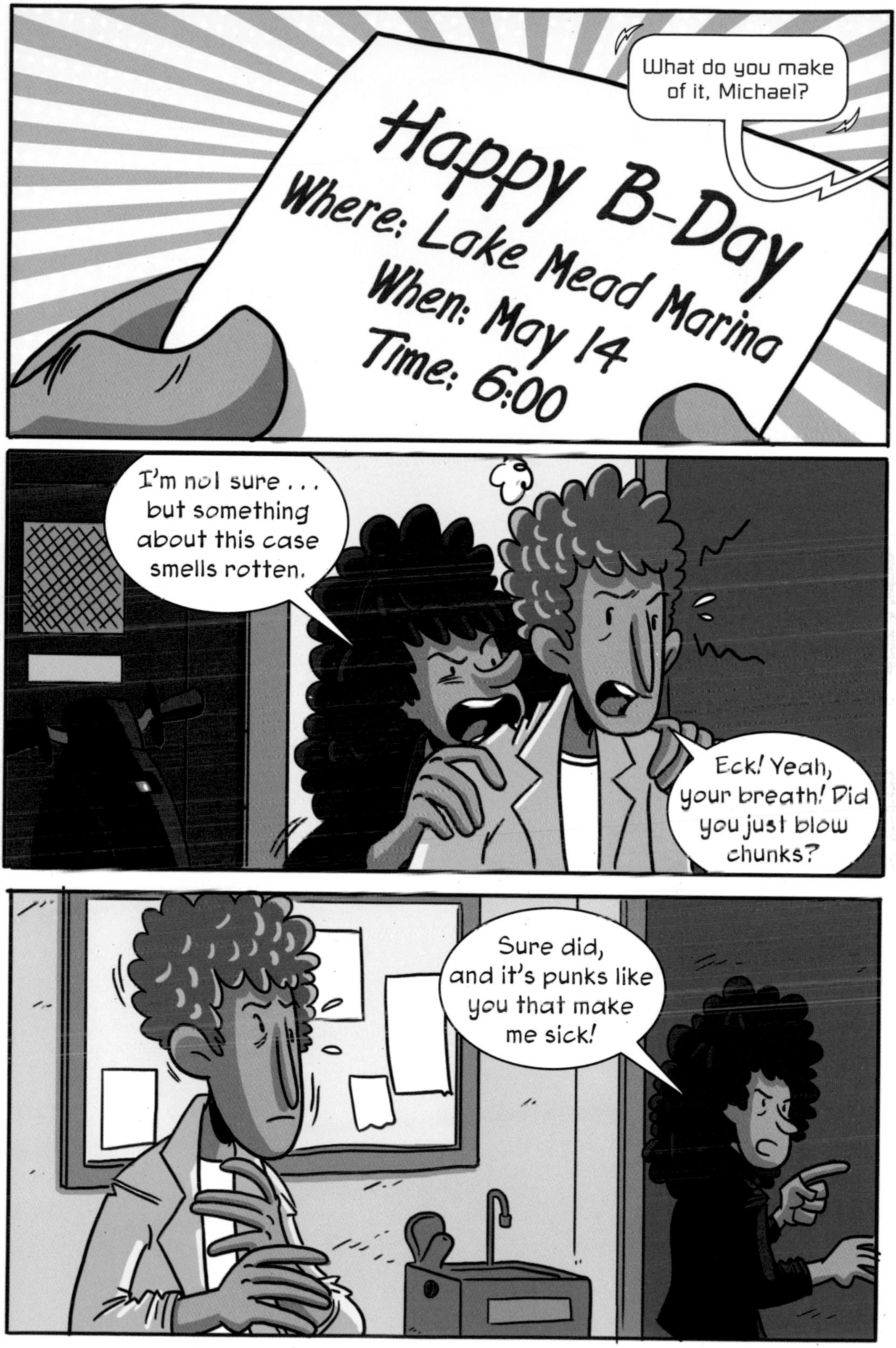
What do you make of it, Michael?
Happy B-Day
Where: Lake Mead Marina
When: May 14
Time: 6:00
I'm not sure . . . but something about this case smells rotten.
Eck! Yeah, your breath! Did you just blow chunks?
Sure did, and it's punks like you that make me sick!

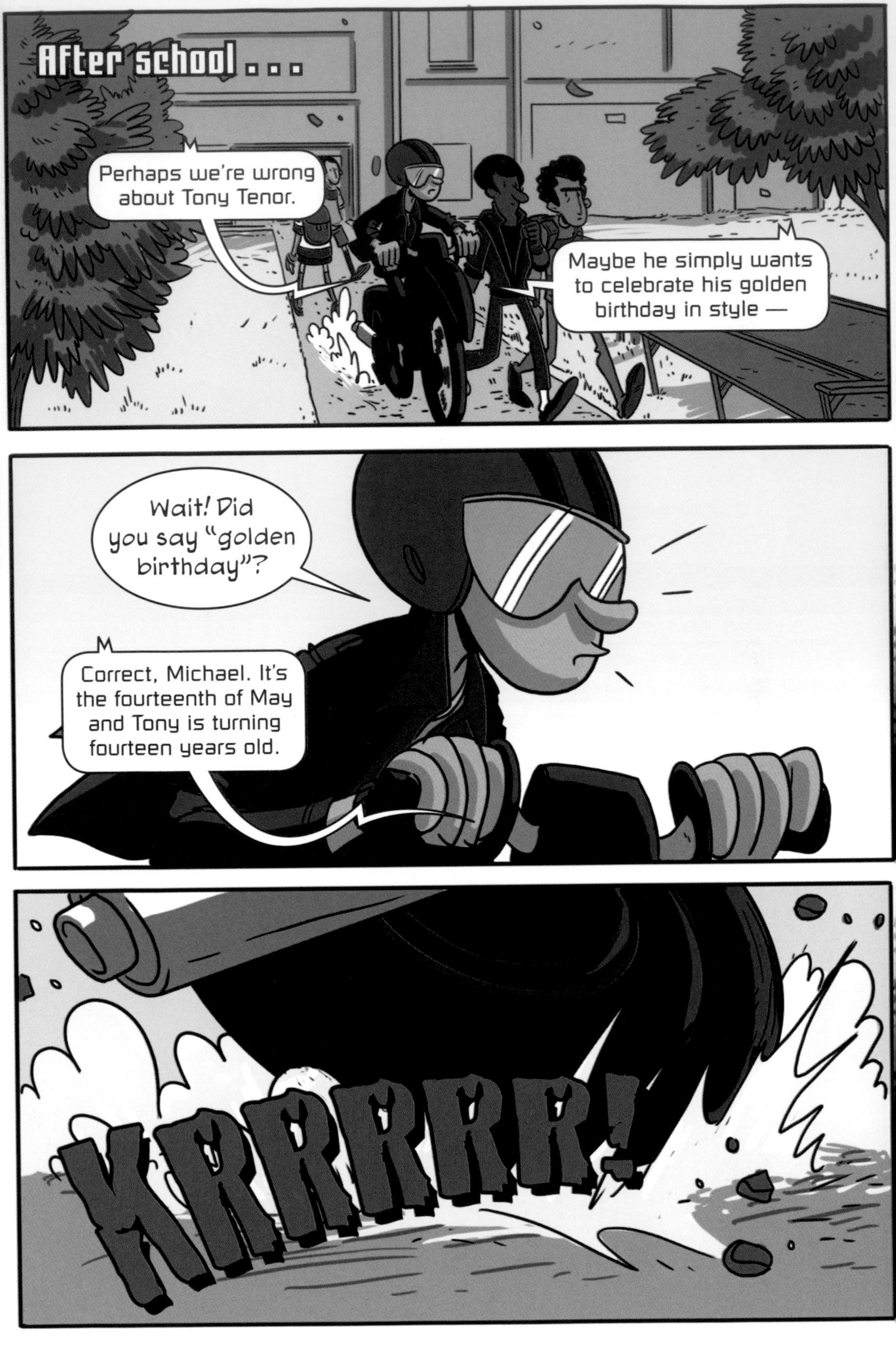
After school . . .
Perhaps we're wrong about Tony Tenor.
Maybe he simply wants to celebrate his golden birthday in style —
Wait! Did you say "golden birthday"?
Correct, Michael. It's the fourteenth of May and Tony is turning fourteen years old.
KRRRRR!

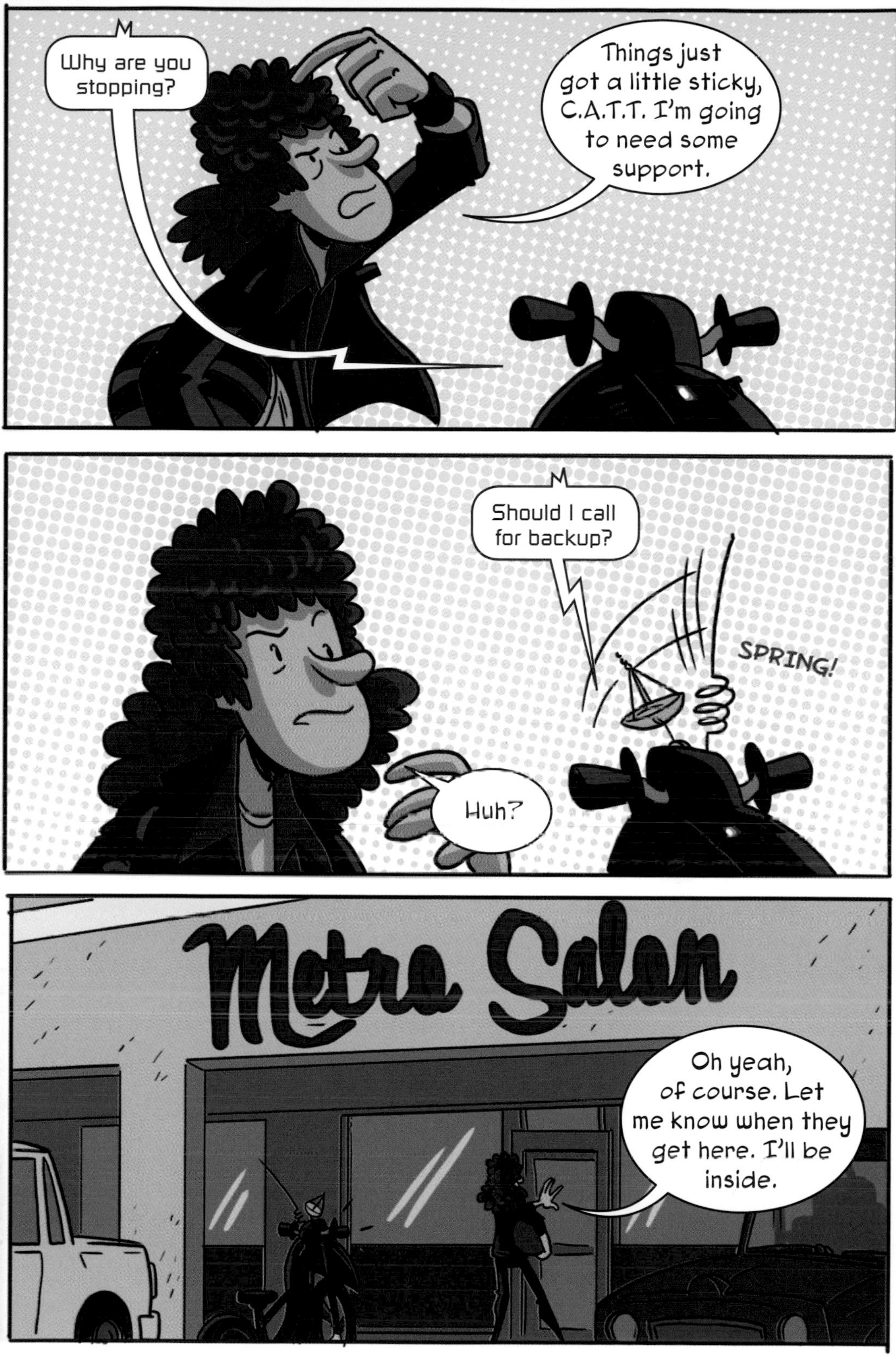
Why are you stopping?
Things just got a little sticky, C.A.T.T. I'm going to need some support.
Should I call for backup?
SPRING!
Huh?
Metro Salon
Oh yeah, of course. Let me know when they get here. I'll be inside.

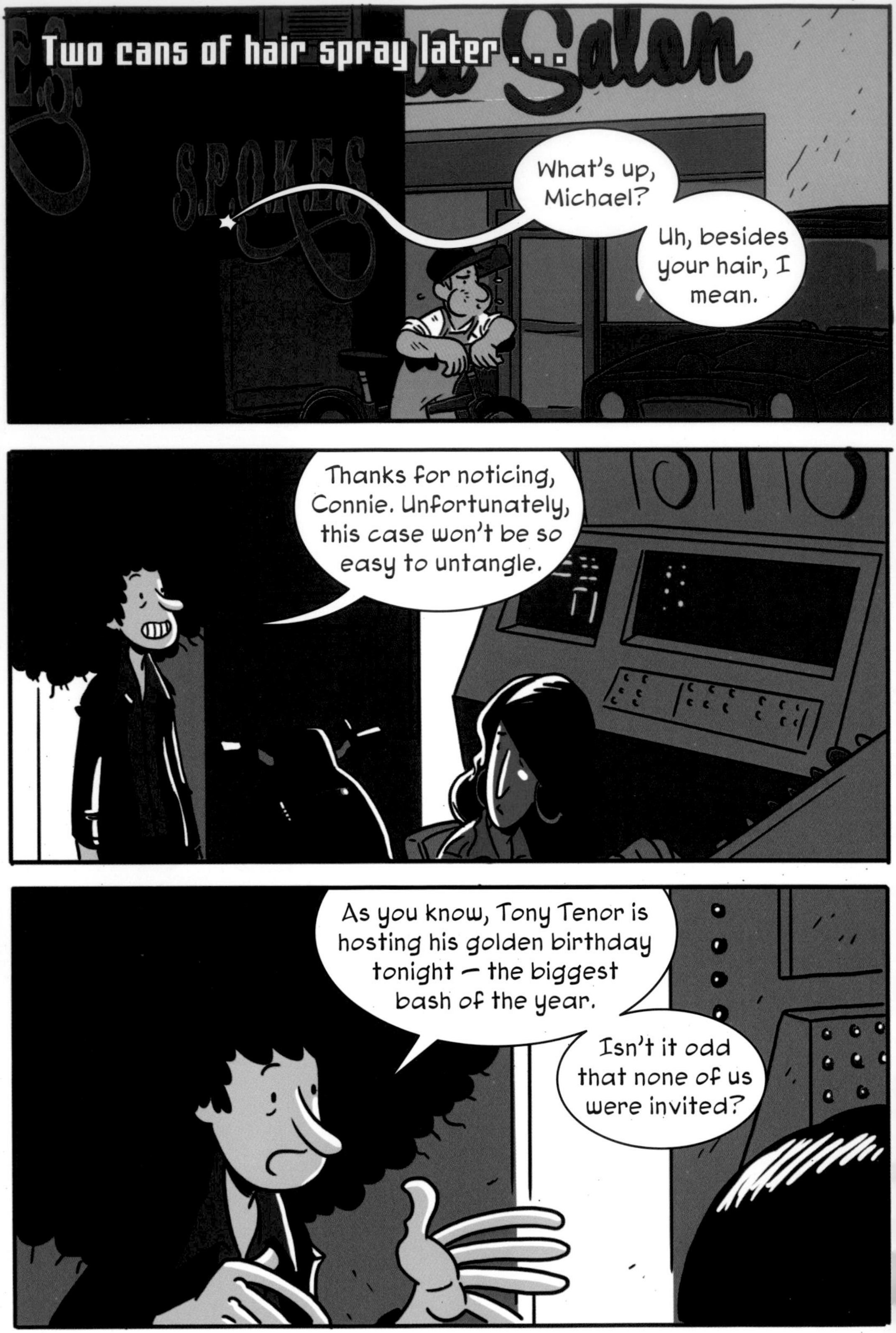
Two cans of hair spray later . . .
What's up, Michael?
Uh, besides your hair, I mean.
Thanks for noticing, Connie. Unfortunately, this case won't be so easy to untangle.
As you know, Tony Tenor is hosting his golden birthday tonight — the biggest bash of the year.
Isn't it odd that none of us were invited?

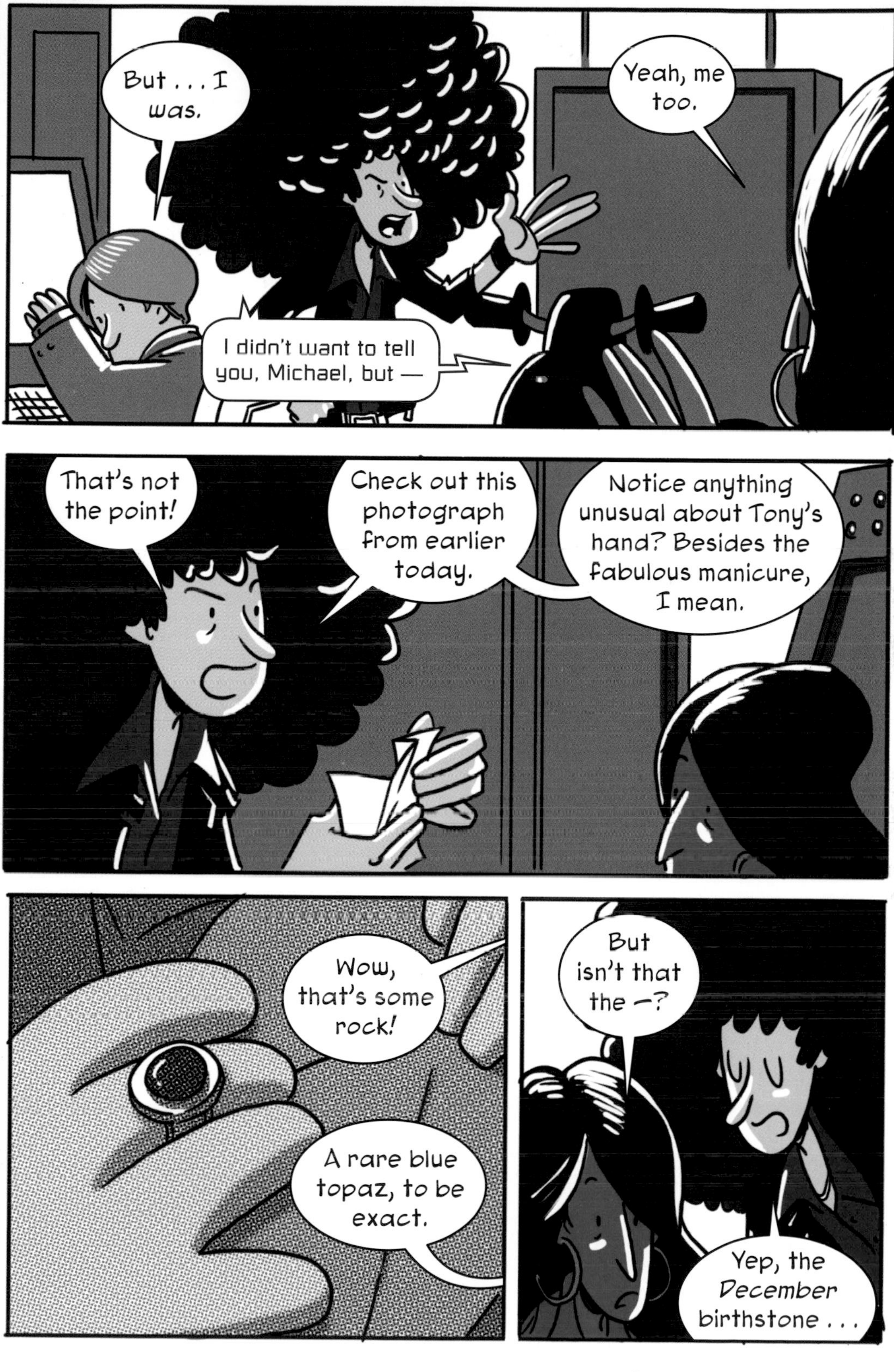

But . . . I was.
Yeah, me too.
I didn't want to tell you, Michael, but —
That's not the point!
Check out this photograph from earlier today.
Notice anything unusual about Tony's hand? Besides the fabulous manicure, I mean.
Wow, that's some rock!
A rare blue topaz, to be exact.
But isn't that the —?
Yep, the *December* birthstone . . .

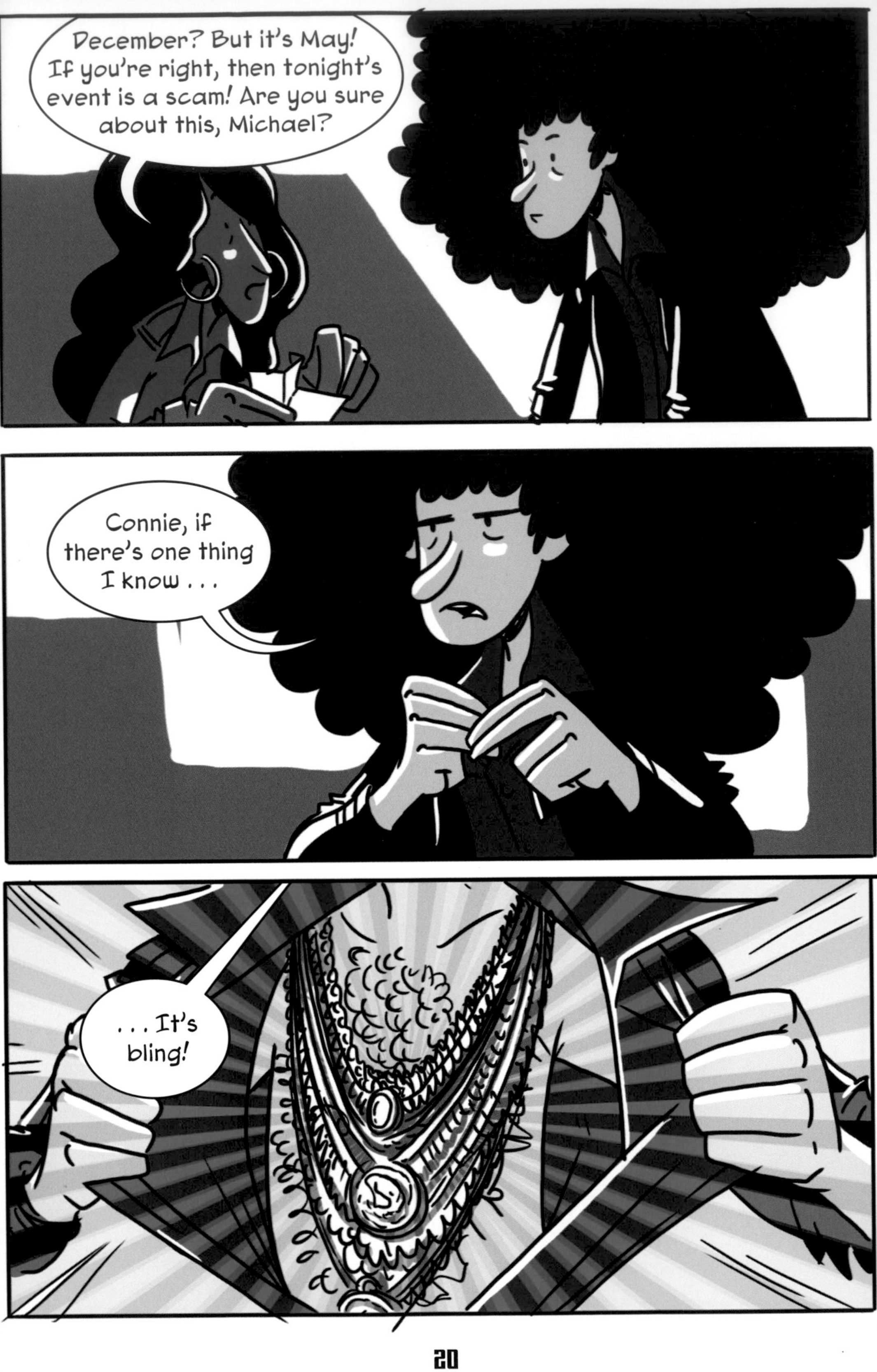
December? But it's May! If you're right, then tonight's event is a scam! Are you sure about this, Michael?
Connie, if there's one thing I know . . .
. . . It's bling!

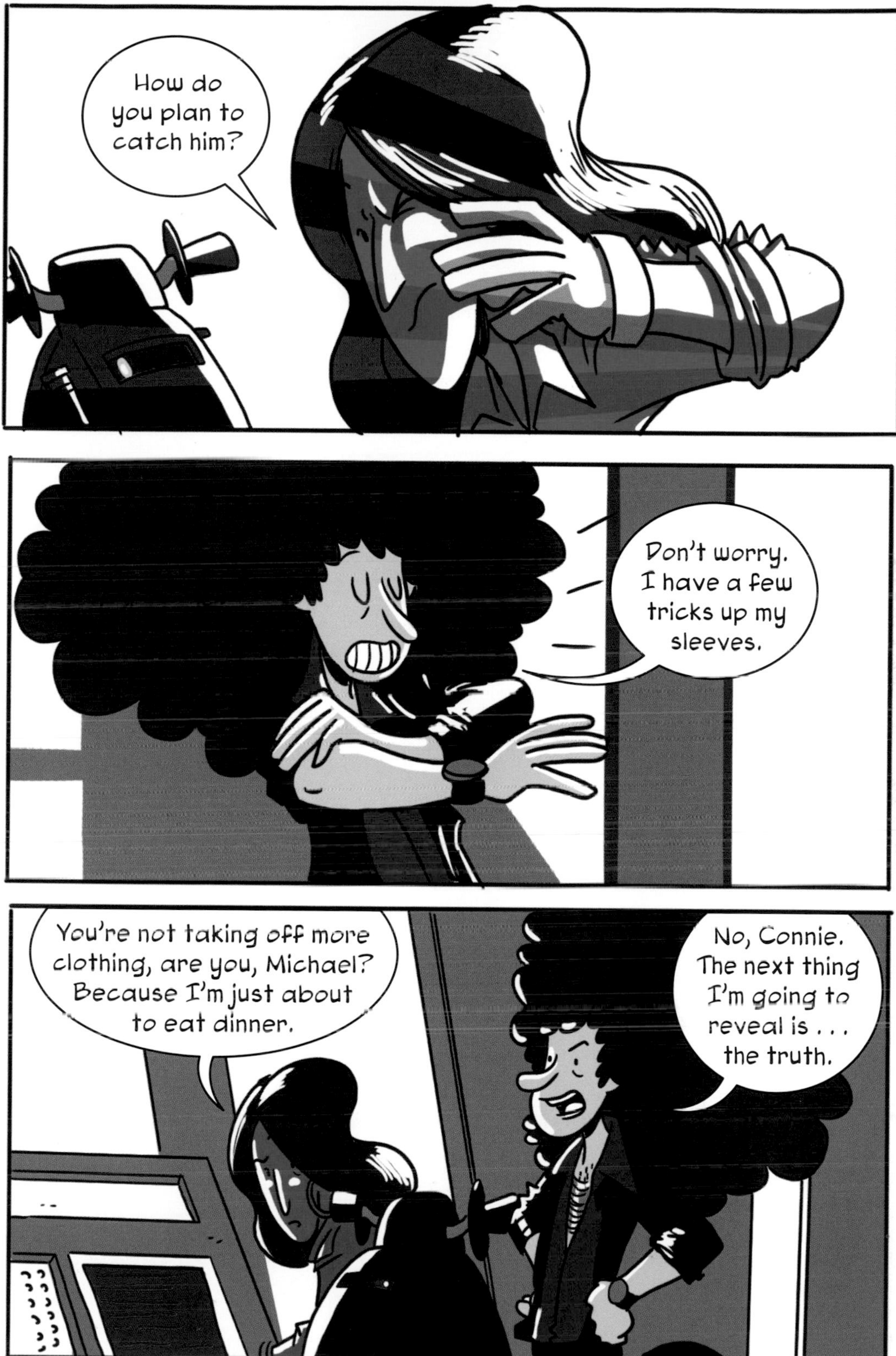
How do you plan to catch him?
Don't worry. I have a few tricks up my sleeves.
You're not taking off more clothing, are you, Michael? Because I'm just about to eat dinner.
No, Connie. The next thing I'm going to reveal is . . . the truth.

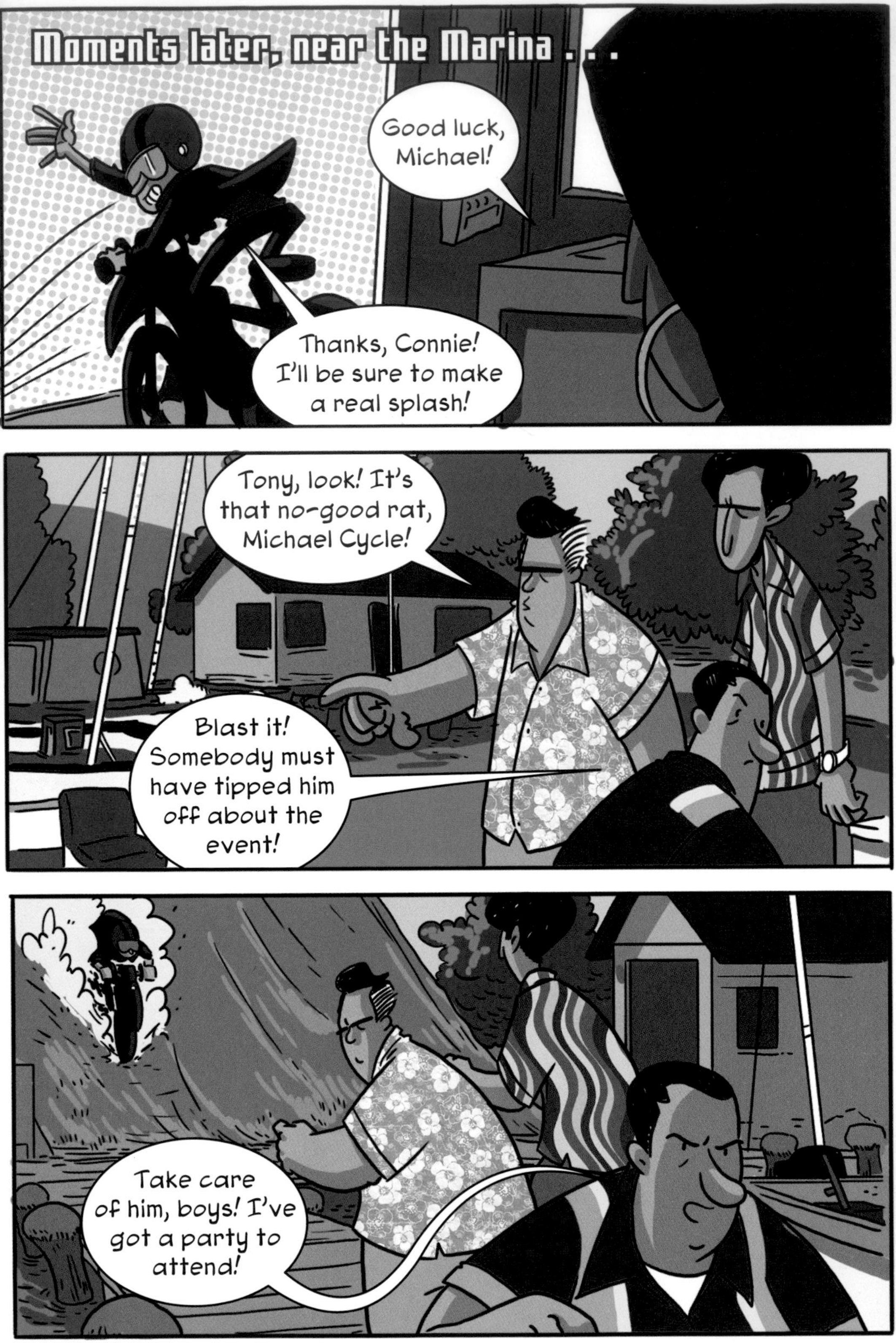
Moments later, near the Marina . . .
Good luck, Michael!
Thanks, Connie! I'll be sure to make a real splash!
Tony, look! It's that no-good rat, Michael Cycle!
Blast it! Somebody must have tipped him off about the event!
Take care of him, boys! I've got a party to attend!

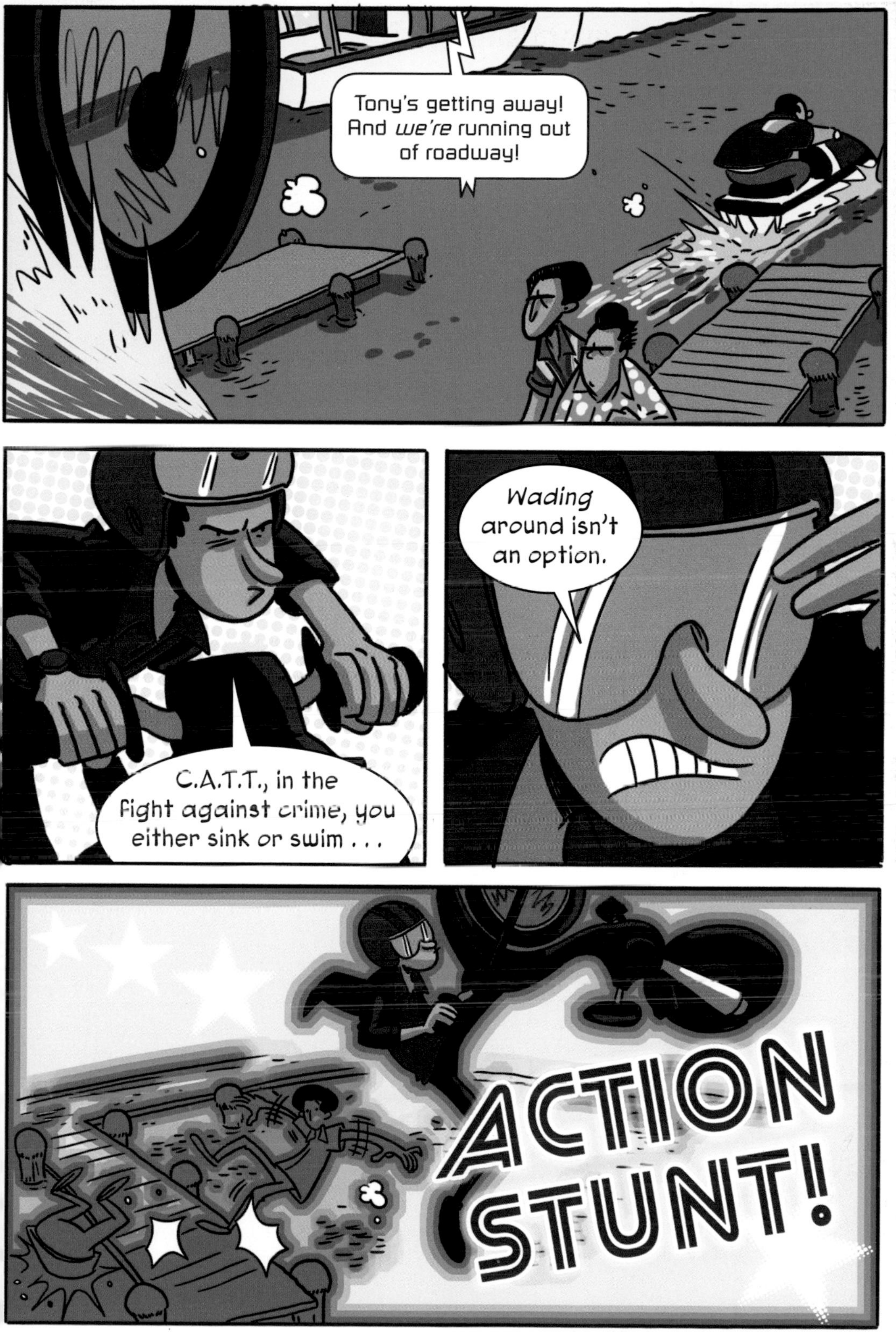
Tony's getting away! And *we're* running out of roadway!
C.A.T.T., in the fight against crime, you either sink or swim . . .
Wading around isn't an option.
ACTION STUNT!

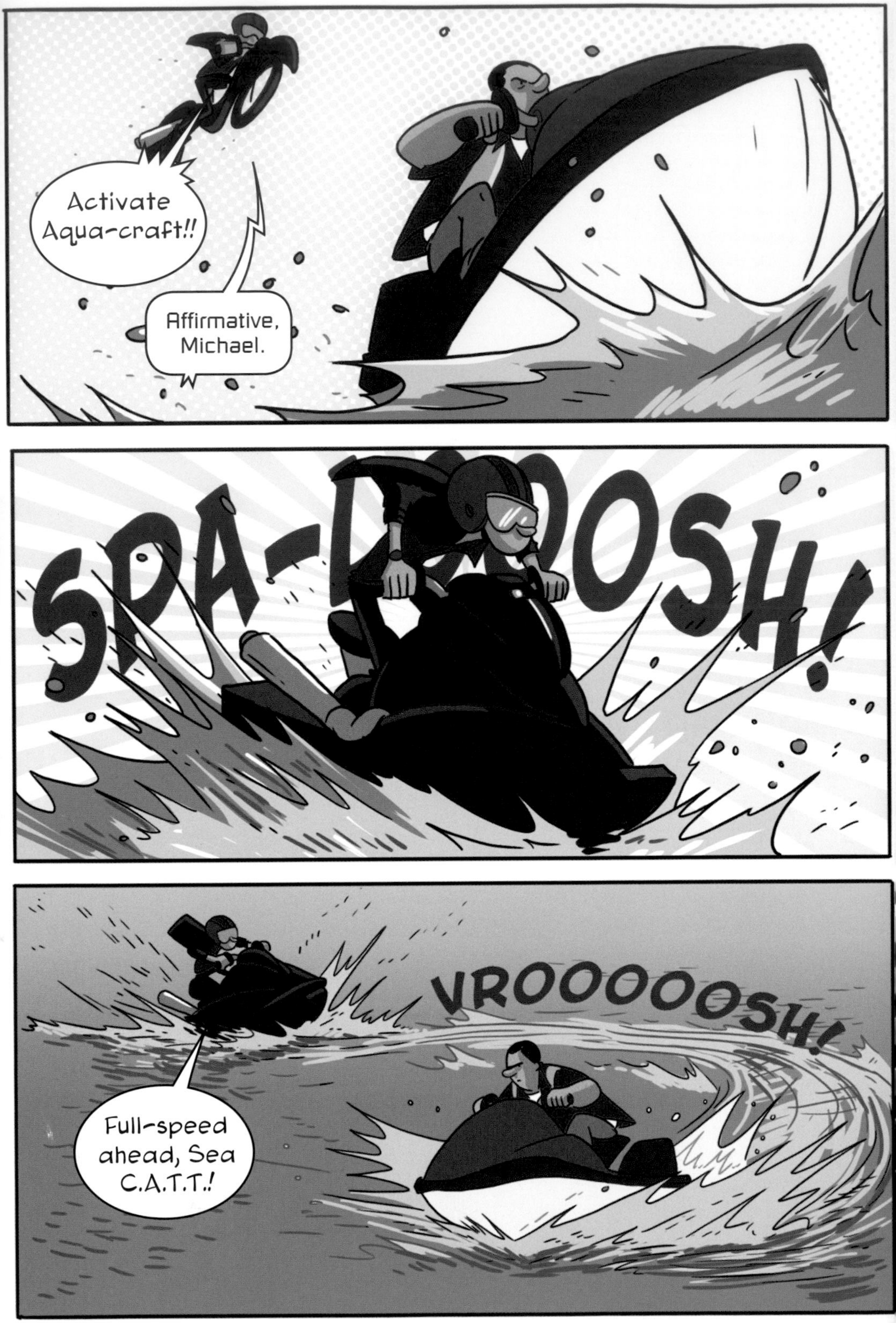
Activate Aqua-craft!!
Affirmative, Michael.
SPA-DOOOSH!
VROOOOOSH!
Full-speed ahead, Sea C.A.T.T.!

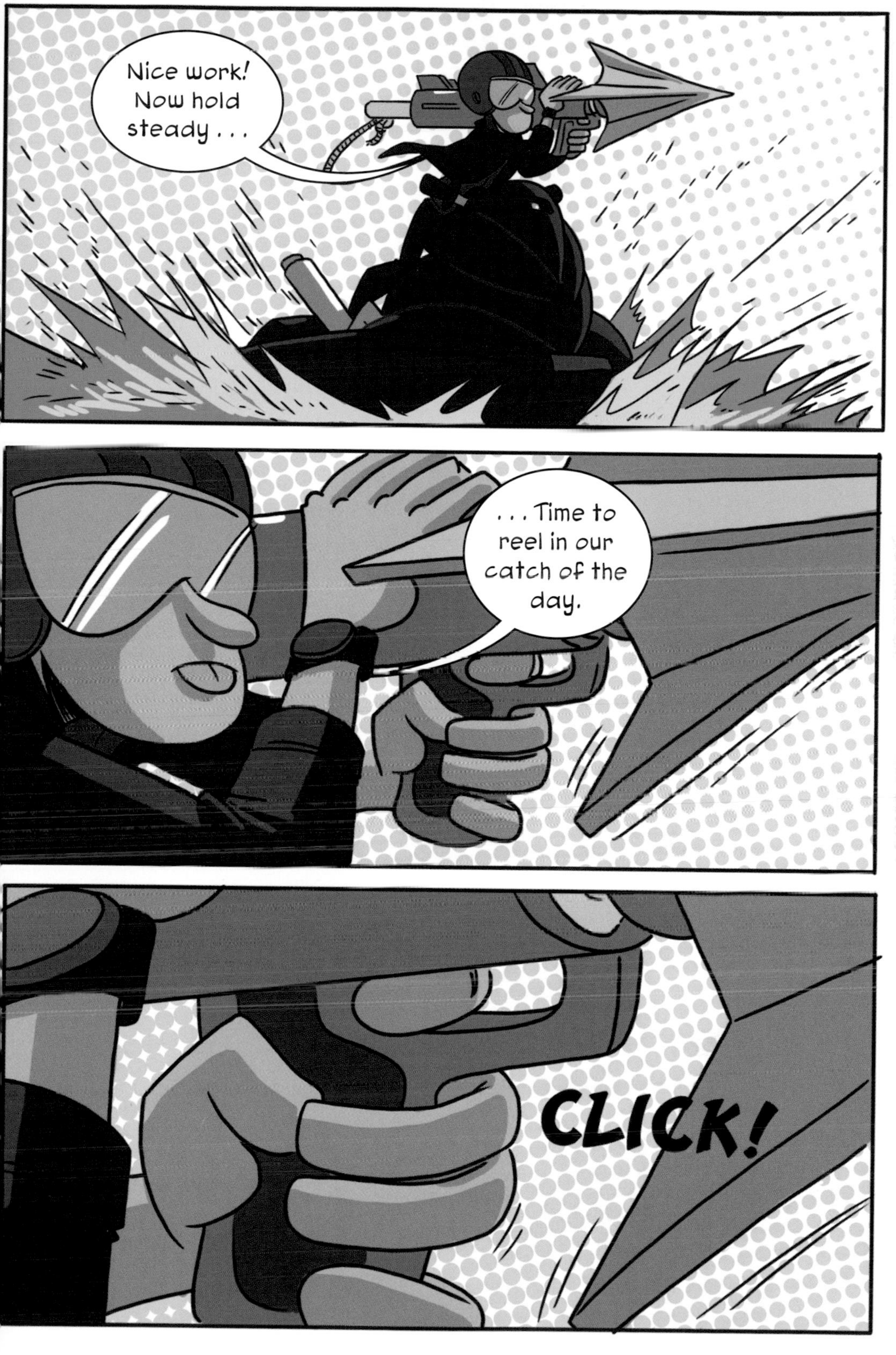
Nice work! Now hold steady . . .
. . . Time to reel in our catch of the day.
CLICK!

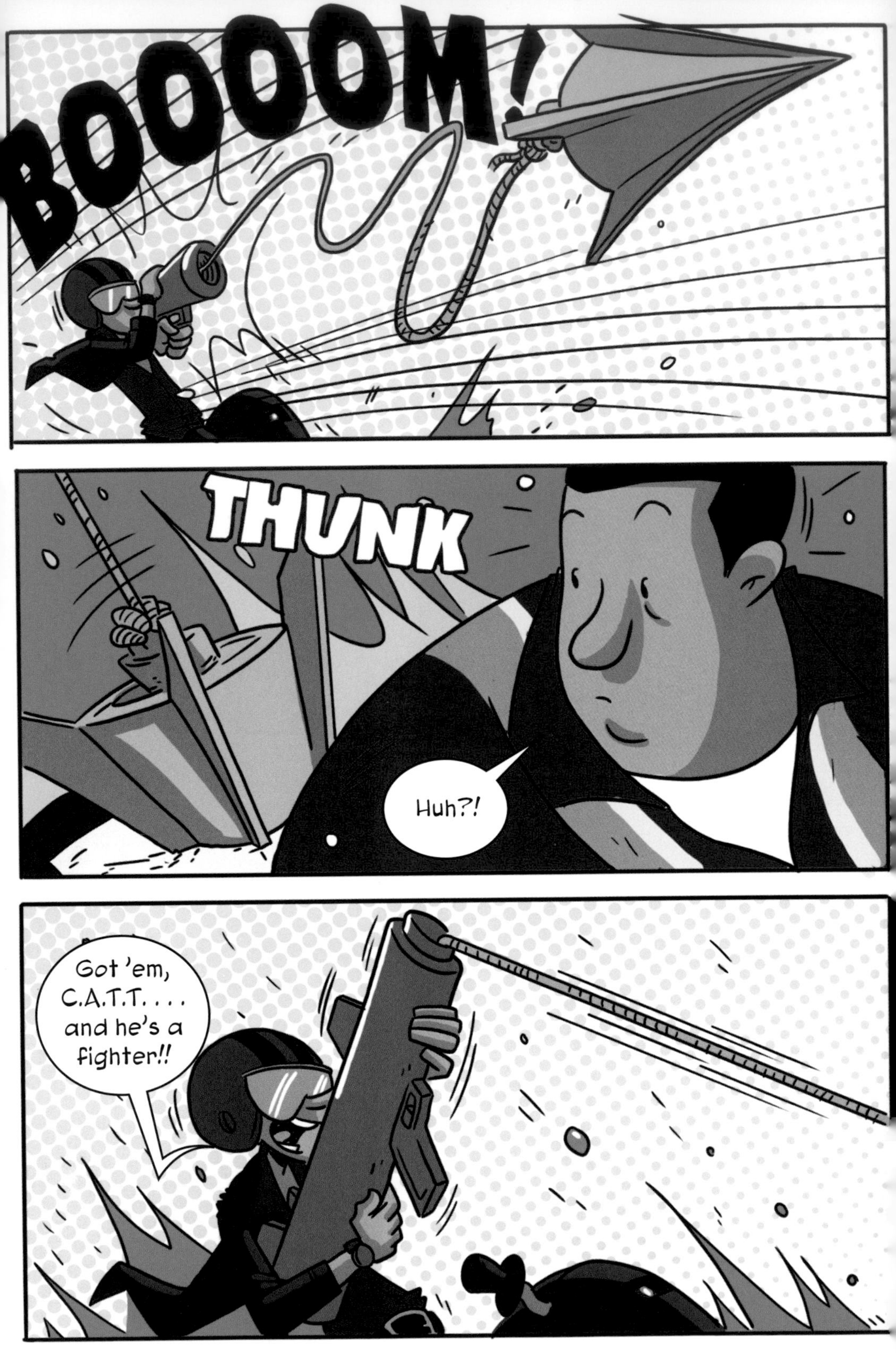
BOOOOM!
THUNK
Huh?!
Got 'em, C.A.T.T. . . . and he's a fighter!!

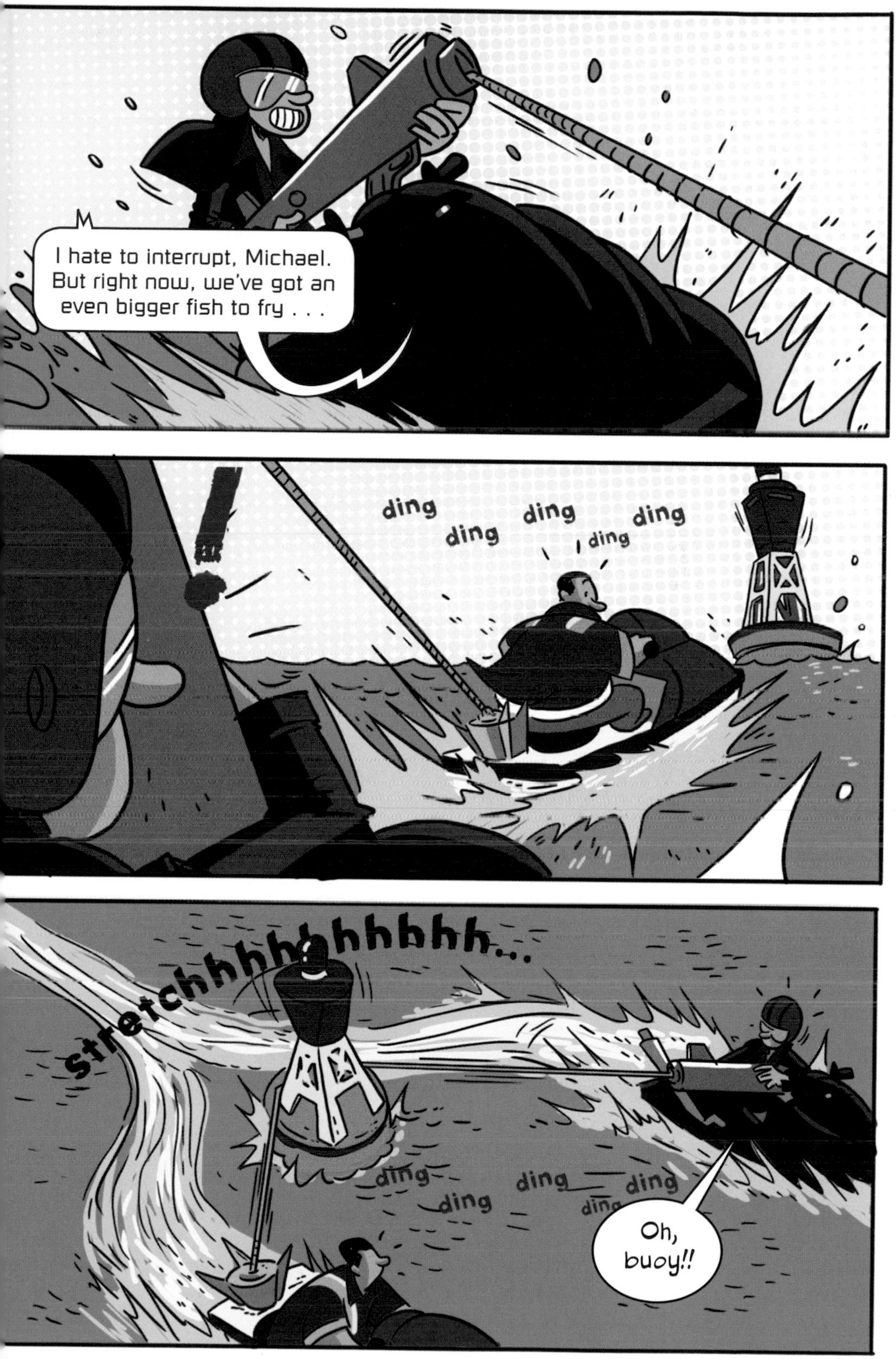
I hate to interrupt, Michael. But right now, we've got an even bigger fish to fry . . .
ding
ding
ding
ding
ding
stretchhhhhhhhhhh...
ding
ding
ding
ding
ding
Oh, buoy!!

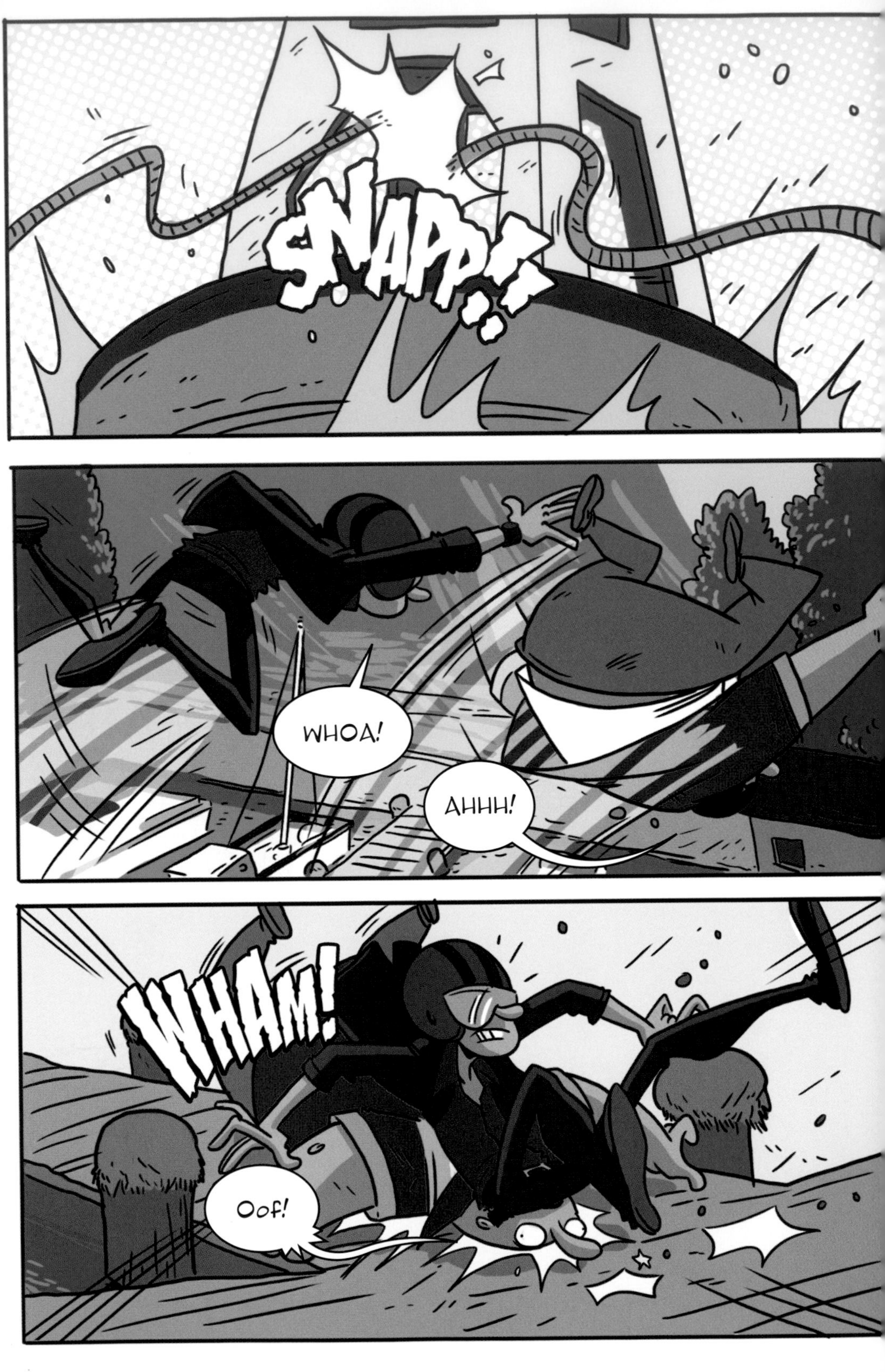
SNAPP!!
WHOA!
AHHH!
WHAM!
Oof!

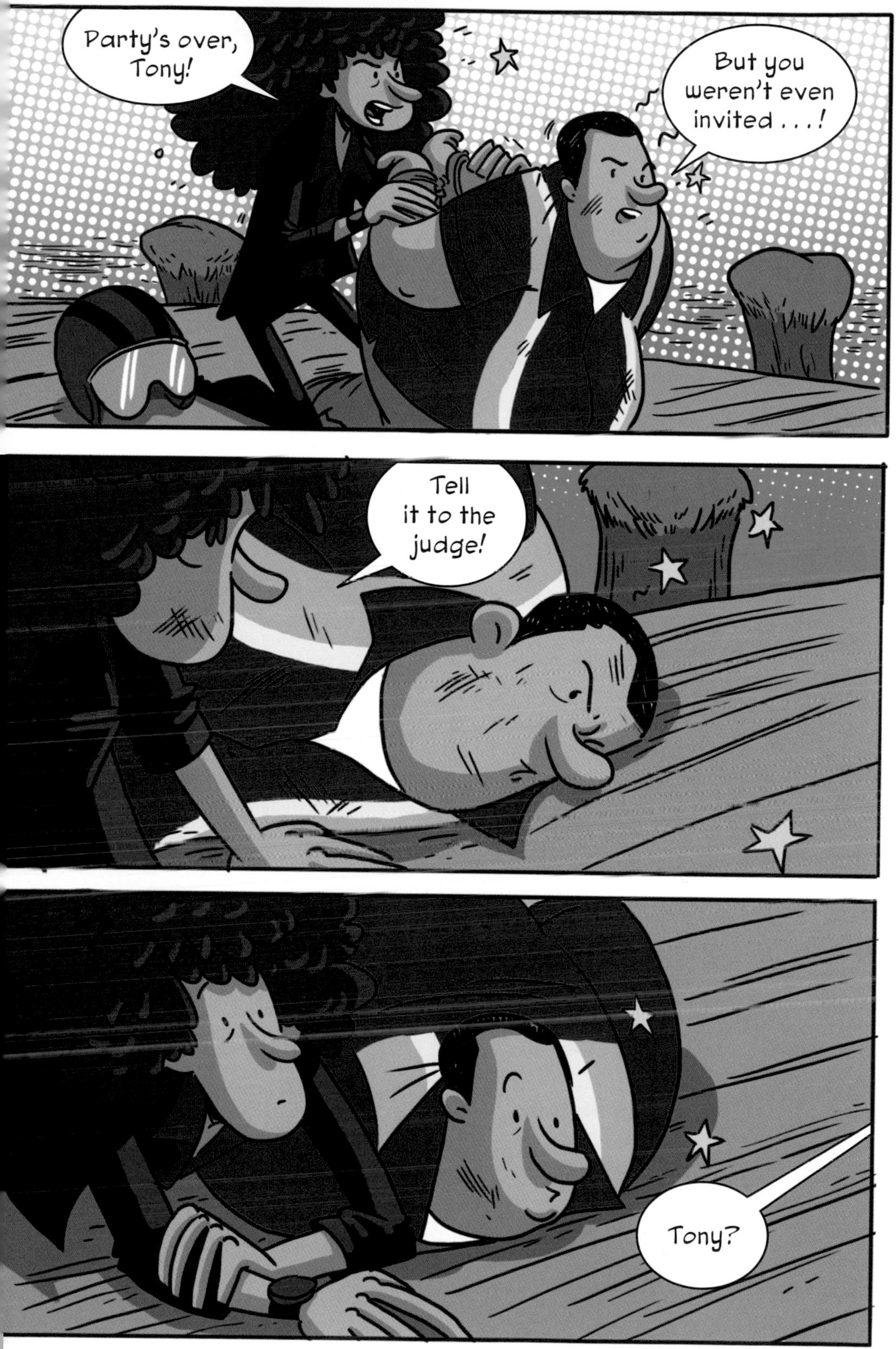
Party's over, Tony!
But you weren't even invited . . . !
Tell it to the judge!
Tony?

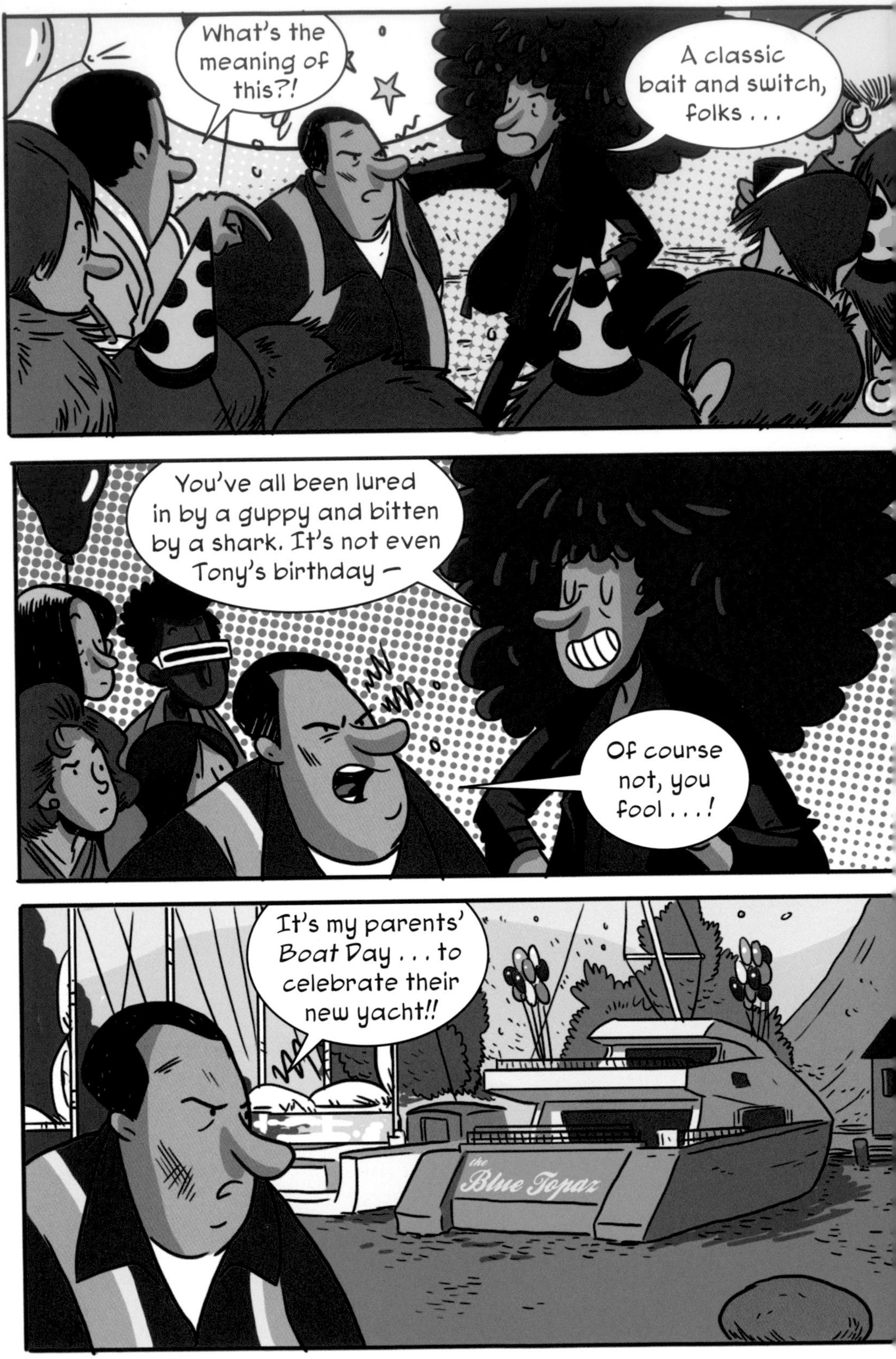
What's the meaning of this?!
A classic bait and switch, folks . . .
You've all been lured in by a guppy and bitten by a shark. It's not even Tony's birthday —
Of course not, you fool . . .!
It's my parents' *Boat Day* . . . to celebrate their new yacht!!
the Blue Topaz

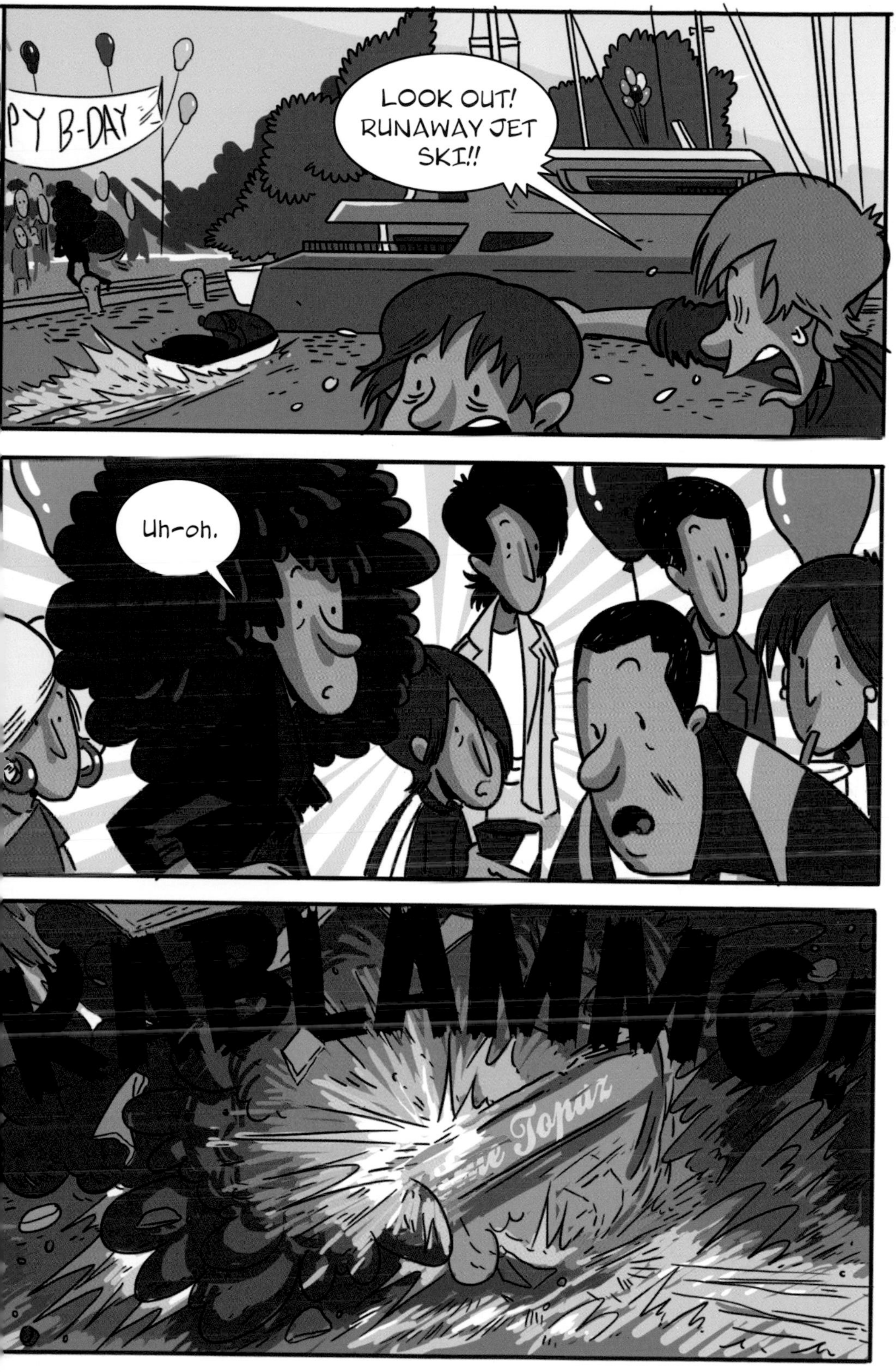
PY B-DAY
LOOK OUT! RUNAWAY JET SKI!!
Uh-oh.
KABLAMMO!
Topaz

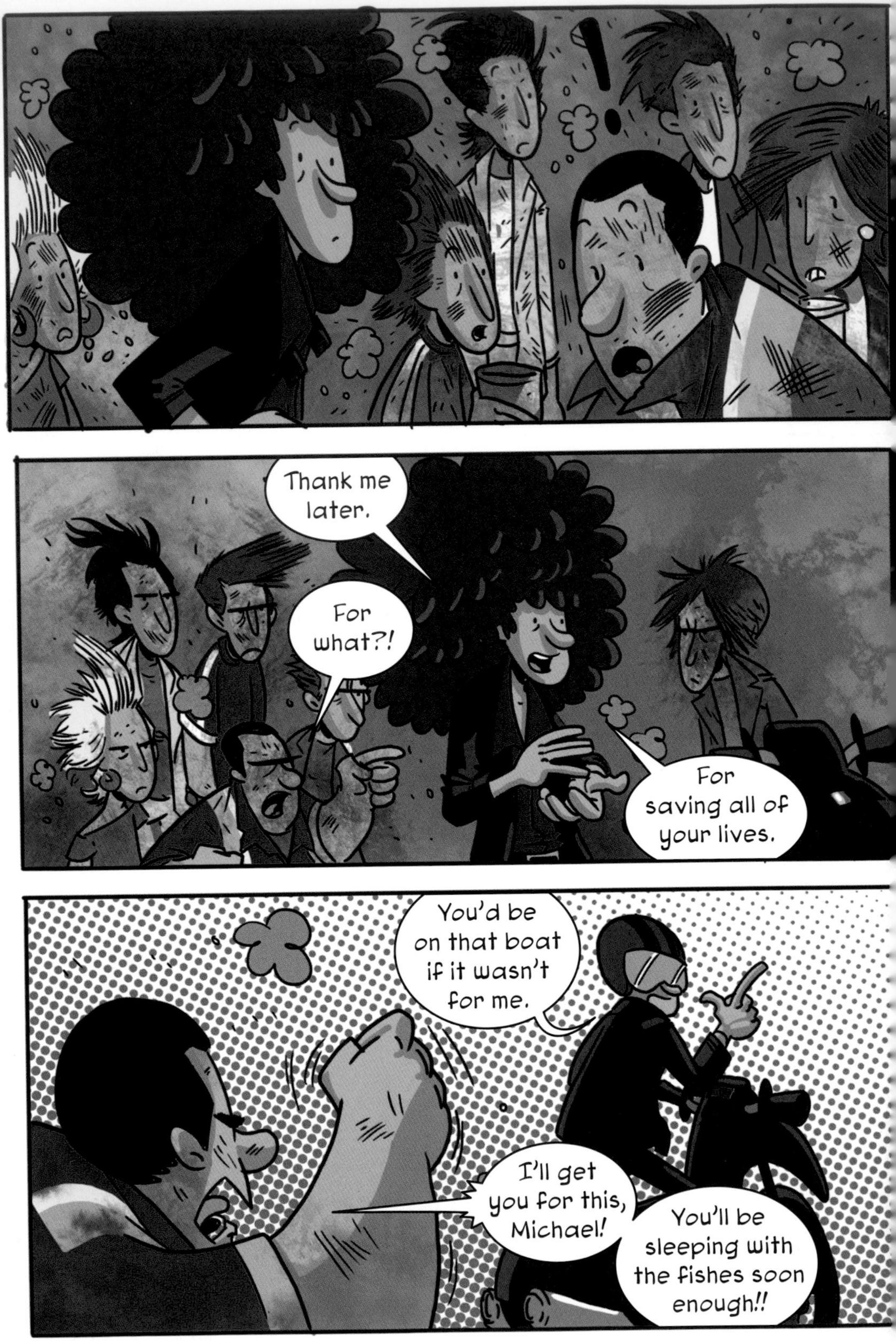
Thank me later.
For what?!
For saving all of your lives.
You'd be on that boat if it wasn't for me.
I'll get you for this, Michael!
You'll be sleeping with the fishes soon enough!!

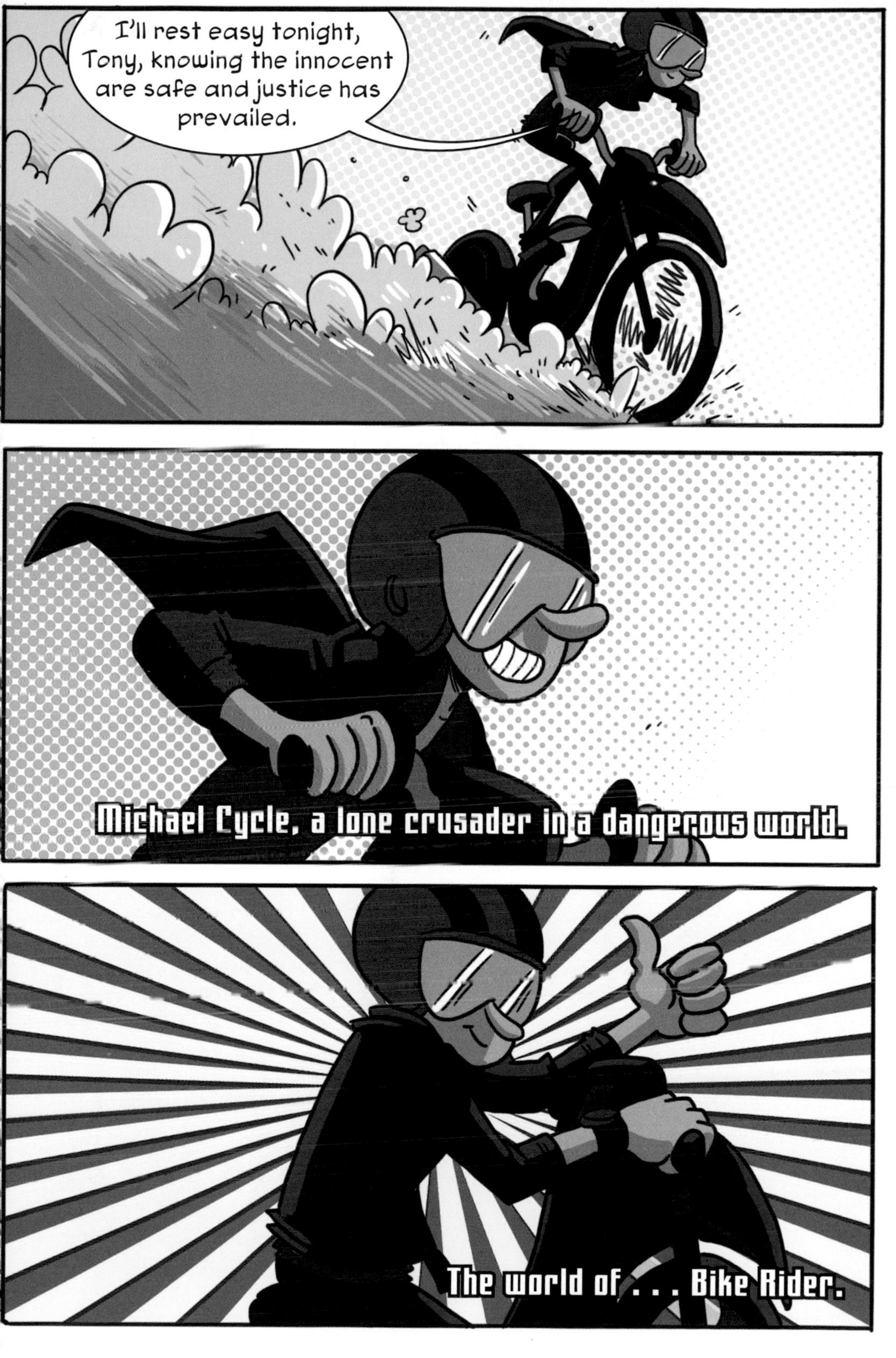
I'll rest easy tonight, Tony, knowing the innocent are safe and justice has prevailed.
Michael Cycle, a lone crusader in a dangerous world.
The world of . . . Bike Rider.

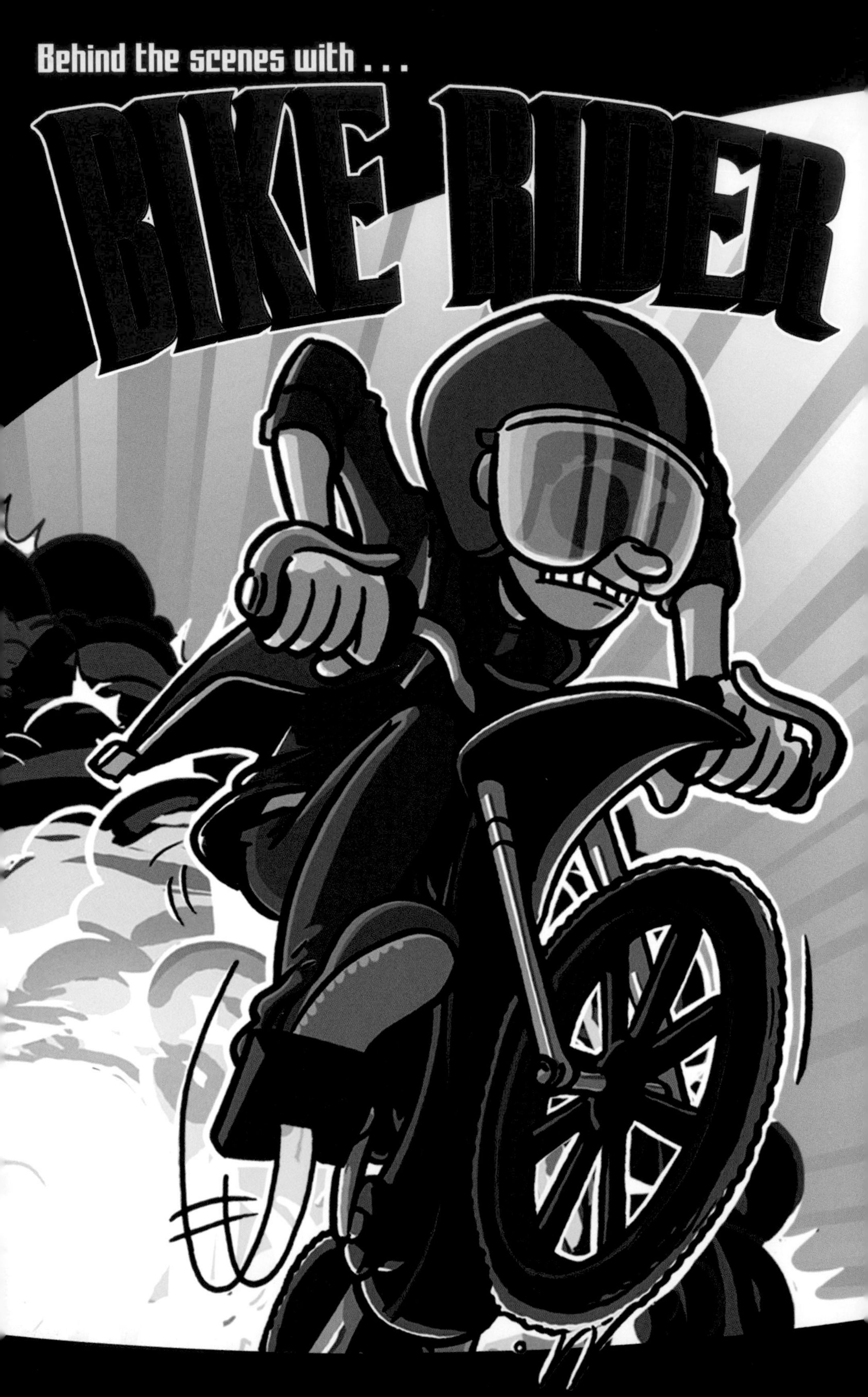
Behind the scenes with . . .
BIKE RIDER

The Origin of . . .
S.P.O.K.E.S.
(Special Protection Of Kids in Education Systems)

On his son's seventh birthday, Senator Ronald Sinclair was charged with ten counts of tax evasion. Although the charges were later dropped, talk-show hosts fed on the scandal, turning against the prominent senator. After failing to secure his bid for reelection, Mr. Sinclair moved his wealthy family to Reno, Nevada. There, he started the grassroots organization, S.P.O.K.E.S., hoping to seize and reform bullies (like those evil talkshow hosts!) before they could graduate from middle school. He appointed his only son, Stephon, to the organization's highest post.

MICHAEL CYCLE and C.A.T.T.

Growing up in Reno, Nevada, Michael Short always had a fondness for the law. At nine years old, he became the youngest crossing guard at T.V. Academy, a position that earned his mother's praise but little respect from his peers. Four years later, Stephon Sinclair approached Michael with a proposition. For accepting the position as the organization's strong arm, Sinclair offered Michael a high-tech, nearly indestructible, talking BMX called C.A.T.T. (Cycle Agency Three Thousand), and a new identity — Michael Cycle (aka Mike Bike), rebel rider.

Up Next . . .

THE NIGHTLY NEWS!

Tonight at ten, we'll give you the inside scoop into the lives of two hardworking individuals, brought together for one totally rad creation . . . the Bike Rider.

CENSORED

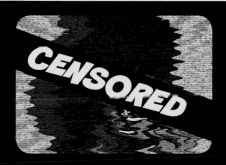

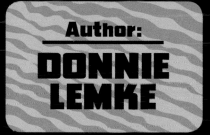

Author:

DONNIE LEMKE

Donnie Lemke works as a children's book editor. He is the author of the Zinc Alloy graphic novel adventure series. He also wrote *Captured Off Guard*, a World War II story, and a graphic novelization of *Gulliver's Travels*, both of which were selected by the Junior Library Guild.

Illustrator:

DOUGLAS HOLGATE

CENSORED

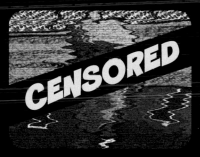

Douglas Holgate is a freelance illustrator from Melbourne, Australia. His work has been published all around the world by Random House, Simon & Schuster, the *New Yorker* magazine, and Image Comics. His award-winning comic "Laika" appears in the acclaimed comic collection *Flight, Volume Two.*

Images have been censored for privacy and protection.

And stay tuned for . . .

TALES OF THE GLOSSARY

affirmative (uh-FUR-muh-tiv)—giving the answer "yes," or stating that something is true

bling (BLING)—shiny and expensive jewelry

felon (FEL-uhn)—someone who has committed a serious crime, such as a burglary or murder

guppy (GUHP-ee)—a tiny freshwater fish popular in home aquariums

manicure (MAN-uh-kyur)—the cleaning, shaping, and polishing of fingernails

scam (SKAM)—a trick to steal someone's belongings

sensor (SEN-sur)—a high-tech device that can detect changes in heat, sound, or pressure

stash (STASH)—something stored or hidden away

surveillance (sur-VAY-luhns)—close watch kept over someone or something

topaz (TOH-paz)—a clear mineral often used as a gem; it is usually a brown or yellow color. Blue topaz is quite rare.

wading (WAYD-ing)—walking through water

yacht (YOT)—a large boat or ship used for pleasure or racing

It will make you think twice about **vocabulary!**

Followed by . . .

QUESTIONS AND PROMPTS

DISCUSSION QUESTIONS

1. Michael Cycle believed that he saved the day at Tony's party. Do you think Bike Rider is a hero? Should he be rewarded for his deeds? Explain your answers.

2. Michael Cycle thought Tony was cheating to get good grades and extra fish sticks. Have you ever caught someone cheating? How did you handle the situation?

WRITING PROMPTS

1. Write your own Bike Rider adventure! What case will Michael Cycle solve next? Will he stop a crime or fall flat on his face? Pretend you're the author and decide his fate for yourself.

2. Bike Rider is based on an 1980s television show. What TV shows do you watch? Pick a show and write your own episode of that program. Once you're finished, find some family and friends to act it out!

Warning: Your brain may swell due to massive amounts of critical thinking.

THE FUN DOESN'T STOP HERE!

Discover more:

- VIDEOS & CONTESTS!
- GAMES & PUZZLES!
- HEROES & VILLAINS!
- AUTHORS & ILLUSTRATORS!

@ www.capstonekids.com

FIND COOL WEBSITES AND MORE BOOKS LIKE THIS ONE
AT WWW.FACTHOUND.COM JUST TYPE IN BOOK I.D.
9781434225375 AND YOU'RE READY TO GO!

▼▼ STONE ARCH BOOKS™

Published in 2011
A Capstone Imprint
151 Good Counsel Drive, P.O. Box 669
Mankato, Minnesota 56002
www.capstonepub.com

ISBN: 978-1-4342-2537-5 (library binding)
ISBN: 978-1-4342-3066-9 (paperback)

Summary: Michael Cycle and his BMX
bike are out to prove that a middle school
Mafioso is up to no good.

Designer: Brann Garvey
Art Director: Bob Lentz
Editor: Donald Lemke
Production Specialist: Michelle Biedscheid
Creative Director: Heather Kindseth
Editorial Director: Michael Dahl
Publisher: Lori Benton

Printed in the United States of America
in Stevens Point, Wisconsin.
092010   005934WZS11